Heir of Monsters

Jessy

J Bailey

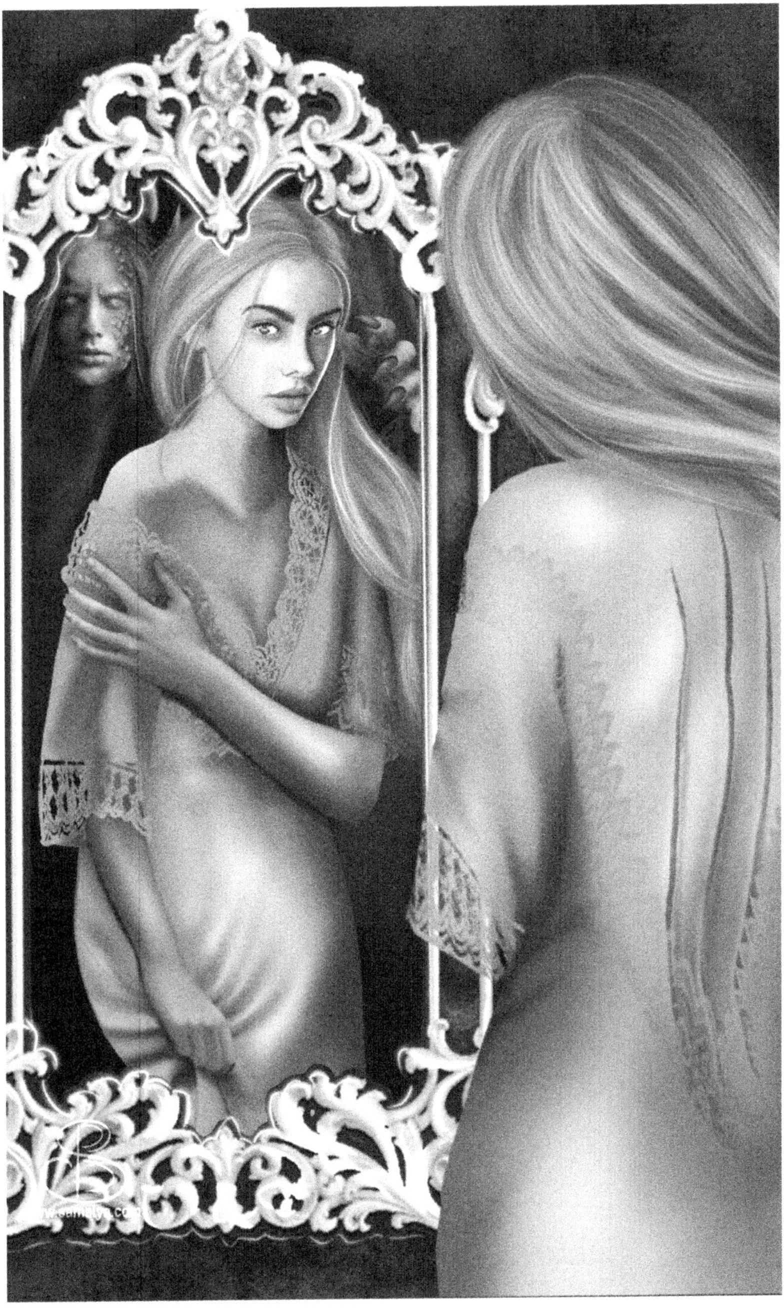

OLD FAE SYMBOLS.

KING	COURT	REBIRTH
WYVERN	SIREN	FAE
QUEEN	CONTROL	

Wyvcelm

The Forgotten Lands

Yoldway City

Junepit City

Ethereal City

Hollowlands

Heir of Monsters.
All Rights Reserved. 2022.

This is a work of fiction. Names, characters, places, and incidents either are the products of the author's imagination or are used fictitiously. Any resemblance to actual persons, living or dead, businesses, companies, events, or locales is entirely coincidental and formed by this author's imagination. No part of this book may be reproduced or used in any manner without the express written permission of the publisher except for the use of brief quotations in a book review.

Edited by Polished Perfection
Cover by Joy Cover Designs
Artwork/chapter heading/background images by Samaiya Art.

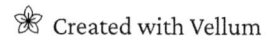

❀ Created with Vellum

CONTENTS

Description	xi
Prologue	1
Chapter 1	5
Chapter 2	33
Chapter 3	41
Chapter 4	58
Chapter 5	73
Chapter 6	98
Chapter 7	113
Chapter 8	133
Chapter 9	147
Chapter 10	168
Chapter 11	183
Chapter 12	198
Chapter 13	216
Chapter 14	233
Chapter 15	253
Chapter 16	273
Chapter 17	295
Chapter 18	316

DESCRIPTION

A monster has stalked me my entire life.
But now I'm hunting him.
My job is to hunt monsters, and I'm damn good at it—until a monster breaks into my apartment in the middle of the night and kidnaps me.
Turns out he isn't just a monster.
He's the Wyern King.
Wyerns, a race feared by everyone, are known to be stronger than the fae who rule my world, and no one has seen them in years until now.
The king needs my help to track down his missing sister from within a city his race is banished from, and I'm the best he can find.

Only, he isn't the only one looking for monsters in Ethereal City.

The Fae Queen's grandson is missing.

Working for fae, monster or not, is risky. Most who are hired end up dead, and I have too much to lose to end up as one of them.

I'm going to find the missing royals and be careful about it, especially with my grumpy boss breathing down my neck and watching my every move.

The Wyern King is cruel, cold, and unbelievably beautiful for a male... and my new enemy.

Heir of Monsters is a full-length paranormal Monster Romance with mature themes. This is a spicy enemies-to-lovers romance and is recommended for 17+.

DEDICATION

*If you once looked for monsters under your bed and
wished you never found one,
this book will make you wish you did.*

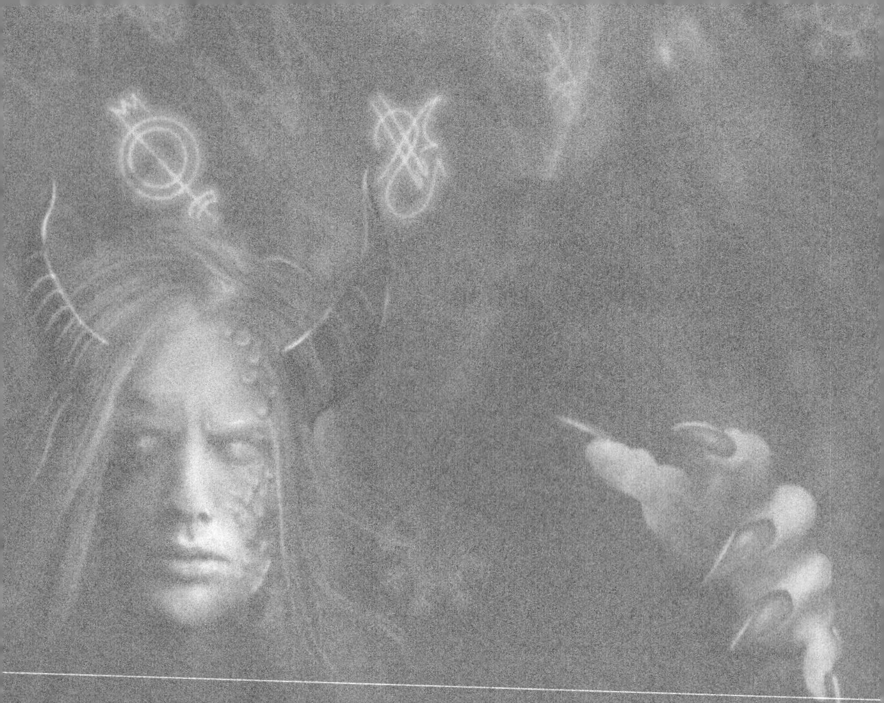

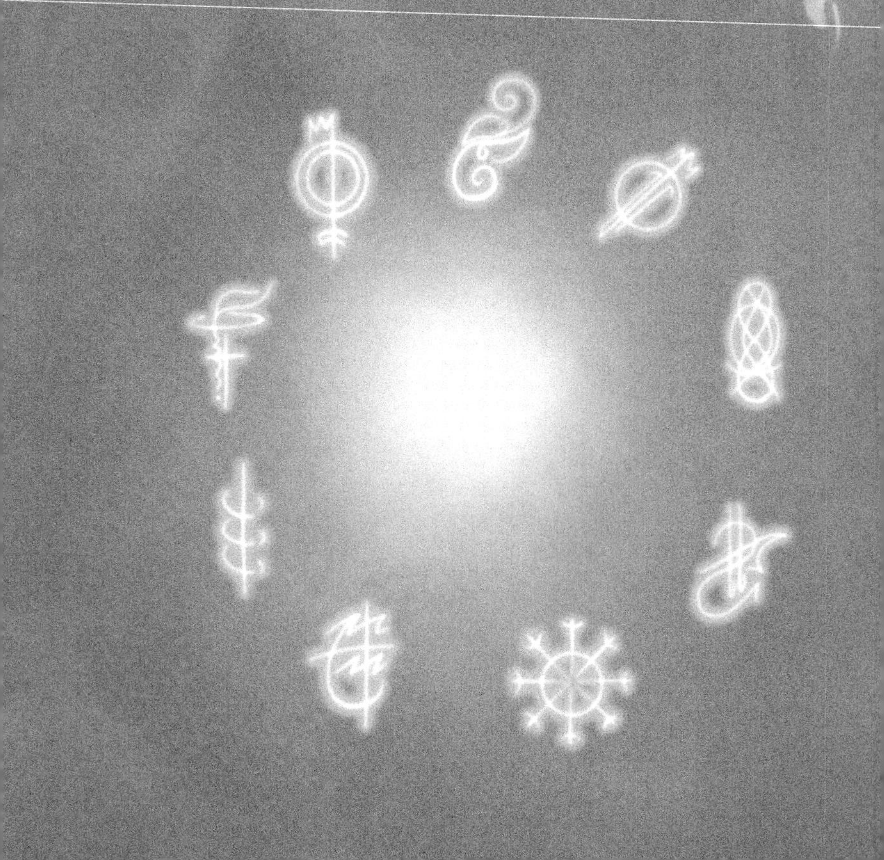

PROLOGUE

"Reborn to mortal life five times over,
Each time, a drop of power taken from the
rift.
Monster cursed is her court,
Royalty protected is her fate,
She will be Queen of the Ruined Clan.
When twelve sit the throne,
She will be born at last.
No longer mortal will she be."

On the edge of the world, in the thick black mountains, a winged male held the mortal body of his beloved as she died once again. His screams and roars shook the snow from the mountain tops and cracked the ground below. But not even he could stop death.

As she died for the fifth and final time, the prophecy began.

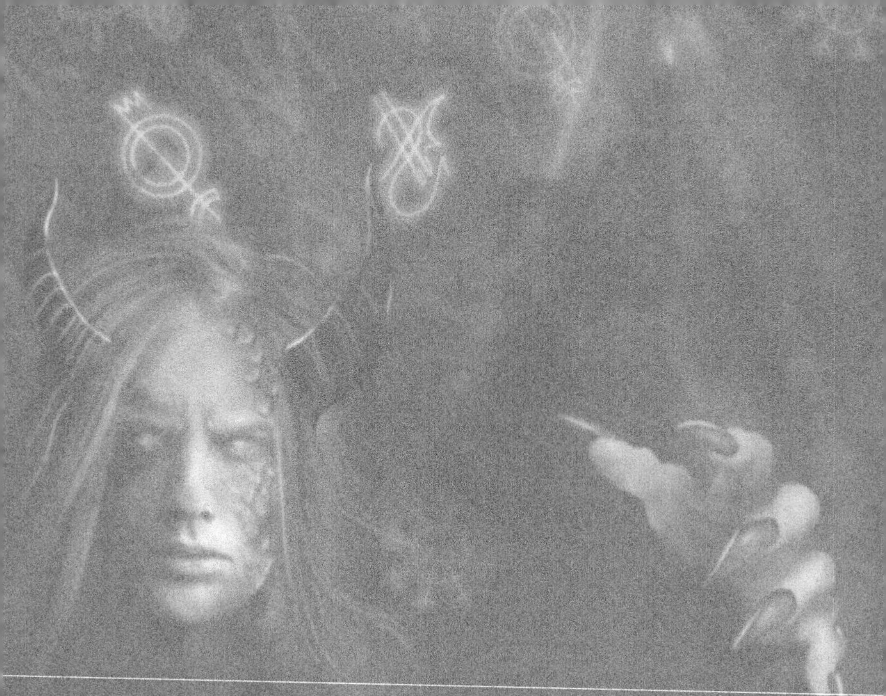

CHAPTER ONE

Monsters are real.

If I needed any more proof than the thing in front of me, then I might be the one going mad in this world. The monster twists its grotesque head back to me, assessing me with its red eyes and mottled skin. It stands at over seven feet, two feet taller than me, and its once mortal-like body is a mixture of wolf and gods know what else. I risk taking my eyes off it for a second to look for my partner, and I catch a flash of red in the darkness behind the monster. I block out the awful stench of the creature and the rattling noise of its bones as it moves while I look for a safe way to take it down without getting us killed.

Clenching my magically blessed dagger in my hand, I whistle loudly. The monster roars loud enough to shake the derelict walls of the ruins before barrelling for me, each step shaking the ground. Like the dumbass that I am, I don't run but charge right back at it to meet it halfway. This plan better work, or I'm so fired. Or dead. I'm not sure which is worse.

"Calliophe! To your left!"

I barely hear my partner's warning shout before something hard rams into the side of me, shooting me into the air. I crash into the stone wall, all the air leaving my lungs as I roll to the floor and gasp in pain.

That hurt.

Blood fills my mouth as I push myself up and pause as I get a look at the giant cat-like thing in front of me. It might have once been a cat, even an exotic and expensive breed, but now it's been warped and changed like the monster behind it. It might even have been his pet. Once.

It lunges for me, snapping a row of sharp yellow teeth, and I narrowly jump to the side before kicking it with my boot. It hisses as I grapple for my dagger in the dust and slash the air between us as a warning as I crouch down. Its eyes are like yellow puddles of water, and I can see my reflection. Despite being covered in dust and dirt, my pink eyes glow slightly, and I look tiny in comparison. Even tiny, with a dagger, can be deadly. If the main monster runs, we might not get another chance to catch it for days, so I call to it, "Over here!"

The strange cat hisses once more, and the hair on its back rises. It straightens with its five strange legs that make it almost as tall as a dog.

A pain-filled female grunt echoes to me, and I clench my teeth. "I need a little help over here, Calli! Or I'm singing and screwing us both over!"

Dammit. I'm going to be the one buying the drinks tonight if she sings. Or worse, explaining this messed up mission to our boss. I'd rather buy the whole entire bar drinks and be poor. I jump on the cat, surprising it and slamming my dagger into its throat as it scratches and bites me before it goes still in my arms. I gently lower it to the ground, closing my eyes for a moment. I love animals, but whatever that was, death was a mercy for it. I pull my dagger out of it, yellow sticky blood dripping down my hand as I run across the ruins to Nerelyth. Somehow, she has gotten herself under a large piece of stone barely propped against a wall where she's hiding, and the monster is on top of it, clawing at the gap and nearly squishing her. I see her wave her arm at me from the small gap, and I sigh. There is only one way to capture a monster. Get up close and personal, and hope it doesn't eat me.

Thankfully, with Nerelyth's distraction, the monster's back is to me as I pull out my enchanted rope and let it wrap around my leg as I run across the ruins and close the gap between us, keeping my footsteps silent. Nerelyth's eyes widen when she spots me, but I don't pause as I leap off a fallen ledge and land on the creature's back, grunting at the impact on my swollen ribs, but my dagger easily slides into its back. Its skin is like goo, and I struggle to hold on as it straightens with a roar, but I lasso my rope around its neck with my other hand. The monster almost screams like a mortal as I let go, sliding down the monster's back and landing in a heap on the ground. I crawl backwards as the rope magically wraps itself over and over around the monster until it ties its legs together and it falls to the side. The rope won't kill it, but it will stay locked up like this for hours, depending on how good the enchantment is.

With a grunt, I stand up and wipe the goo off my hands and walk over to where Nerelyth is still hiding. I tilt my head and look down at my partner, who has her eyes closed. "It's sorted now."

Nerelyth is lying face up under the stone, her red hair splayed around her. Her chest is moving fast as she finally opens her eyes and looks over at me, arching an eyebrow. "Thank you. Again," I tell her. "We might have fucked up." I offer her my hand as she brushes the dust off her leather clothes. "Any chance you love me for saving you and you will explain it to the boss?"

"Not a chance," she chuckles as I help her climb out, light shining in from the bright sun hanging over us. We both stop to look over at the monster, who is trying to escape the rope.

"Third one this month. Where do you think they are coming from?"

"Not a clue," I mutter, eyeing the monster suspiciously. "I'm not sure M.A.D. even knows where the hybrids are coming from. They still happily send us out with no warning that this wasn't a normal job. Assholes."

She shrugs a slender shoulder, picking out flecks of dust from her flawless waist-length dark red hair that matches the red curls of water marks around her cheek that go all the way down her neck to her back. I'm certain I look much worse than she does, and I'm not even attempting to take my hair out of my braid to fix it. "The money is worth it."

Lie. I've been in the Monster Acquisitions Division, aka M.A.D., for three years, and the pay has never been good compared to the other divisions, and we both know it. Like everyone says, you have to be literally mad to make it in M.A.D. for more than a month.

Most enforcers, like us, are sent here as a punishment for fucking up. I had no choice but to take this job, as it was all I could get with my background, lack of money, and young age when I started at only eighteen. I glance at my partner of just one year and wonder again why a siren is working in one of the shittiest divisions in Ethereal City. Sirens are one of the wealthiest races, and the few I know work at the top of the enforcers. Not at the bottom, like us, which makes me question my friend's motives for being here with me once again. "Drinks tonight?"

"You know it," she says with a friendly smile and tired viridescent green eyes. "I'll send a Flame to get some enforcers down here to take him in. You get back to the office and good luck."

I groan and send a silent prayer to the dragon goddess herself to save me.

~

I HEAD across the busy market street and look up at the Enforcer Headquarters as I stand on the sidewalk. The streets around me are filled with mortals and supernaturals heading to or from the bustle of the market to buy wares, food or nearly anything they want. The market hill is right at the top of the city, and it's the biggest market in Ethereal City. Fae horses wait by their owners' carts at the side of the main path, and I eye a soft white horse nearby for a moment and admire its shiny coat.

From this point, I can see nearly all of Ethereal City, from the elaborate seven hundred and four skyscrapers right down to the emerald green sea and the circular bay at the bottom of the city. Ethereal City was created over two thousand years ago, and the bay is even older than that. Dozens, if not hundreds, of ships line the ports, and they look like sparkling silver lines on the crystal green sea. Beyond that, the swirling seas of the largest lake in the world stretch all the way to the horizon and far beyond.

Most of Wyvcelm is this land, wrapped around the jeweled seas between Ethereal City and Goldway City on the other side. There are a few islands off the mainland, and one of them I want to go to one day—when I'm rich enough. Junepit City, the pleasure lands. I shake my head, pushing away that dream to focus on the Jeweled Seas, and I think of Nerelyth every time I see it.

The Jeweled Seas are ruled by the Siren King, and no one ever travels through them unless you are a siren, escorted by sirens, or want to die. Nerelyth told me once about how going through the fast, creature-filled rapids and the narrow cliff channels makes it nearly impossible to survive for long unless you know the way and can control the water. Above the sea level is worse as enchanted tornadoes reach high into the sky, swirling constantly over the waters controlled by the sirens themselves. That's why they're one of the richest races in Wyvcelm, because if the sirens didn't control the tornadoes, they would rip into both Ethereal City and Goldway City, ending thousands of lives. But they are not richer than the fae who rule over our lands and pay them to keep us safe.

I turn to my right, looking up at the castle that looms above the entire city. Its black spiraling towers, shining slate roofs and shimmering silver windows make it stand out anywhere that I am in the city. It was made that way, to make sure we always know who is ruling us. The immortal Fae Queen. Our queen lives in that palace and has done her entire immortal life. Thousands of years, if the history books are right and our longest reigning queen to date. She keeps us safe from the dangers outside the walls of the city, from the Wyern King and his clan of Wyerns who live over in the Forgotten Lands. They are the true monsters of our world.

A cold, salty breeze blows around me, and I shiver as I pull myself from my thoughts and look back up at the building where I go every single day. The Enforcer Headquarters, one of twelve in the city, and they all look the exact same. Symmetrical pillars line the outline of the two-story building that stretches far back. Perfectly trimmed bushes make a square around the bottom floor, and three staircases lead up to the platform outside the enormous main door. All of it is black, from the stone to the bushes, except for the white door, which is always open and always guarded by new junior enforcers. I walk up the hundred and fifty-two steps to the doors, and both the enforcers nod at me, letting me in without needing to check my I.D. I'm sure they have heard of me—and not in a good way. My list of fuckups is a mile long.

I glance at the young enforcer, a woman with cherry red lipstick and black hair, and wonder why she chose to sign up to be an enforcer. I doubt she was like me, fresh out of the foster system and left with no other decent options but this. Many don't want this job, and with the right schooling, they don't have to take it. It's hard work and long hours… and we die a lot. I've been lucky to skirt death myself a few times, and each time, I thank the dragon goddess for saving me. I smile at the junior enforcer and walk into the building, across the shiny black marble floors and up to the receptionist, Wendy, who sits behind a wall of glass and a small, tidy oak desk. I like Wendy, who is part witch, but I don't hold that against her. Her black hair is curled up and pinned into a bun, and she is wearing a long blue skirt and a white chemise top. "Hello, Calliophe. I missed you yesterday during the quarter term meeting."

"Sorry about that. Monster hunting and all," I say with a genuine smile even if I'm not sorry at all for missing another boring meeting. "Is he in there?"

She nods at the steps by the side of her office that lead up to the only full floor office on the top level. All the rest of us have our offices below his. The boss made sure that he had the only room above when he was transferred here a year ago. Her dark, nearly black eyes flicker nervously. "Upstairs. He's not in a great mood tonight."

"Brilliant," I tightly say and take a deep breath. "Thanks, Wendy. See you around if I survive the boss's bad mood."

"Good luck," she whispers to me before I walk to the stairs and head up to the top level. I'm glad I took the time to quickly get changed into a black tank top and high-waisted black jeans. My pink hair flows around my shoulders to the middle of my back, reminding me that I need a haircut soon.

When I get to the top of the stairs, I pause to look over the gigantic space that I'm rarely invited into, noticing how it smells like him. Masculine, minty and cool, which suits the space he has claimed. Massive floor-to-ceiling windows stretch across the back area, giving magnificent views of the fae castle upon the hill and the rest of the city below it. The towers, the small buildings, the people are easy to see from this vantage point. The sun slowly sets off in the distance, casting cascades of mandarin, lemony yellow and scarlet red light across the tips of buildings and across the shiny black floor. The light spreads across my boots as I walk into the room and finally look over at him. He is sitting at his desk, the single piece of furniture in this whole massive space, and on the desk is a Flame.

Flames are small red gnomes that use flames to travel from one place to another, and in general, are useful pests. The city is full of them, and for a coin, they will send a message for you. I've heard that you can ask the Flames to send anything you want, even death, to another, but it comes with a price only the dragon goddess herself could bear. They are ancient creatures and not to be messed with. I wouldn't dare ask for more than a message, and not many would. The Flame looks back at me with its soulless black eyes, and then he disappears in a flicker of flames, leaving embers bouncing across the desk.

Merrick looks up at me with his gorgeous dark grey eyes, and the room becomes tense. Some would say his eyes are colorless, but I don't think that's true. His eyes are a perfect reflection of any color in the room, and there are others that claim his grey eyes suggest he has angelic blood. Which is laughable. The Angelic Children, a race so rare we hardly ever see them, are said to be endlessly kind.

There's nothing nice or kind about Merrick Night. My boss. His dark brown hair is perfectly gelled into place, not a stray daring to be wrong, and it's much like the expensive black suit, the perfect black tie, flawless white shirt tucked into black trousers he wears, all of it expensive. He doesn't wear the enforcer leathers, magically made material, and he has never explained why.

I stop before his desk and cross my arms.

"Do you want to explain yourself, or should I start, Miss Sprite?"

His deep, cocky, arrogant voice irritates me as we both know he knows what happened—and why. But fine, if we are going to play this game.

I resist the urge to glower at my boss, not wanting to get fired, as I lift my chin. "I'll start, boss. We were told it was a simple monster on the loose on the left side of the city—Yenrtic District. It was suggested that an exiled werewolf had murdered mortals, and they called us to take him in. That was all that we were told, and we went to hunt him as per our job. He might have been part werewolf once, but he wasn't anymore when we found him. He was a hybrid, twisted and changed into something indescribable, but I'm sure we can go take a visit if you wish to see it."

"That won't be necessary, Miss Sprite," he coldly replies, running his eyes over me once.

I grit my teeth. "It was a difficult mission. We were underprepared for it, and none of the usual tactics for taking down a shifter worked. It went a little wrong from the start, and I do apologize for that."

"A little wrong," he slowly repeats my answer.

Here we go.

He stands up from his desk and walks over to his window. "Come with me."

I reluctantly follow him over, standing at his side as he towers over me. I hate being short at times. "A little wrong is when you make a small mistake that no one notices what you did and it doesn't attract attention. M.A.D. is known for discreetly dealing with supernaturals who have turned into monsters, for the queen. Destroying two buildings would suggest it went very wrong and quite the opposite of what your job stands for."

"Boss—"

"And furthermore, my boss is breathing down my neck to fire you. He is questioning why two of my junior associates have somehow managed to destroy two fucking expensive buildings. Explain it to me. Now, Miss Sprite."

"Technically, the monster destroyed the buildings when it had a tantrum and reacted badly to the enchanted wolfbane," I quietly answer.

"If you were struggling, you should have sent for help," he commands. "Not taken it on yourself with a new enforcer."

"We didn't have time, or it would have escaped and killed more mortals," I sharply reply. "Isn't that the real job? To save lives?"

An awkward silence drifts between us, and I steel my back for his reply. "You're meant to be instructing your partner on how to responsibly take on monsters. What you did today was teach her that you can take on a hybrid, alone, and somehow survive by the skin of your teeth. When she goes out and repeats your lesson alone, she will be hurt. Even die."

Guilt presses down on my chest. "But, boss—"

"Yes, Miss Sprite?" he interrupts, challenging me to say anything but *I'm sorry* with those cold grey eyes of his. When I first met Merrick Night, I thought he was the most beguiling mortal I'd ever met. Then he opened his perfectly shaped lips and made me want to punch him.

I look away first and over the city, the last bits of light dying away over the horizon. "There's been so many of these hybrid creatures recently, all over Wyvcelm. I have contacts in Junepit and Goldway City who told me as much. Where are they coming from? What caused them to be like that?"

"That is classified, Miss Sprite," he coolly replies. Basically, it's well above my pay grade to ask.

"It's probably not safe for everyone to go out in twos on missions like this anymore," I counter.

"Your only defense is that you secured the monster without Miss Mist using her voice," he says with a hint of cool amusement. "That would have been a real fuckup for us all to deal with."

Fuckup would be an understatement. The sirens' most deadly power, among many, is their enchanted voice when they sing the old language of the fae. Instantly, she would lure every male in the entire vicinity towards her, monster or not, and they would bow to her alone. Mortal females like me would be left screaming for the dragon goddess to save us, holding our hands over our ears, begging for death. Her voice stretches for at least two to three miles, and only a full-blooded fae can resist it. I've only heard it once, and personally, I never want to hear it again. I can still hear it now, like an old echo that draws me to her, a flash of the old power of the sirens who used to rule this world before the fae rose to power.

"Am I fired or can I leave, boss?"

He links his fingers, leaning back in the chair, which creaks. "I'm itching to dock your pay for this. But I won't. Not this time. You can go."

"Thank you," I say sarcastically and turn on my heel.

"Miss Sprite?" I stop mid-step and look back at him. "Don't make me regret being lenient on you today. You should know better."

I nod before turning away. "Fucking asshole," I whisper under my breath. He's not supernatural, and I know he can't hear me, and it's not like I can actually call him that to his face. Then I'd be fired for sure. Still, I'm sure I hear him chuckle under his breath.

I rush down the steps and say goodbye to Wendy before leaving the enforcement building and going to the Royal Bank on the other side of the market. I withdraw my day's pay, wincing that it's not nearly as much as I need, but a few hundred coins will sort everything out, and I'll work a double shift at the end of this week so I can eat for the rest of the week.

After making my way through the market and grabbing some dried meats, I head into the complex where my apartment is, listening to the old tower creak and groan in the wind. My apartment is four hundred and seven out of eight hundred flats in the entire building, and it is owned by the Fae Queen, like everything else. I'm lucky I got a place here, in a decent side of town, and it is everything I've worked towards for a very long time. I take the steps two at a time until I get to the hundred level. The corridor is littered with bikes, toys and plants, like every family level.

I knock twice on door one hundred and seven before opening it up with my key and heading inside.

"It's just me," I shout out as I feel how cold it is in here and flick on the magical heating. The weather is always changing so quickly. Some say it's the old gods anger that changes the weather from hot to cold all within a day. I'll pay that bill later, either way. "Louie?"

"Here," Louie shouts back, and I follow his shout to find him in the open-plan kitchen-living area, also where he has a small bed pushed up at the one side. The walls are cracked, the cream paper peeling off, but it's the same in most of the apartments. Louie is sitting on the bed, throwing an orange ball in the air and catching it over and over. Louie catches the ball one more time before sitting up, brushing locks of his black hair out of his eyes.

"How was school?" I question, leaning against the wall.

"Boring and predictable. Mr. French told me I was too smart for the class and suggested I join the fae army. Again," he tells me, and my heart lurches for a second until I see him chuckle. "I'm not crazy. Obviously."

After the age of ten, any male or female can join the fae army and be trained to fight for the queen, but they have to take the serum. The serum is an enchanted concoction that turns any mortal into a full-blooded fae and forces a bond between whoever takes it and the queen. Meaning that no one who takes the serum can ever betray her. I once thought about joining the fae army myself when things were rough and I was starving, but I will never forget the other foster kids in the homes who died from the serum. Roughly ten percent survive. I will never let Louie take a risk like that. Not even for the riches and security and the promise of power that the Fae Queen offers up.

I'm lost in my thoughts. I don't even notice Louie climb off his bed and come over to me. His eyes are like molten silver, just like his father's were. "You look tired."

"Hello, good to see you, too. How's your mom today?"

"The same," he quietly says, walking past me and opening the door to her bedroom. His mom was once a foster mom of mine, and the only one alive. I look down at her in her bed, her thin body covered in an unnatural blue glow as she lightly hovers off the bedsheets. Five years ago, we were attacked by the monster who has hunted me my entire life. Five years ago, her mate jumped in front of her to save her life, they smashed through a wall, and she hit her head on the edge of a door. My foster dad was the only reason I became an enforcer—because he was one. The Enforcer Guild paid for this apartment and a magically protected sleep until she can be woken, not that we can afford to do that, and the Guild's sympathy only stretched so far.

This was my eleventh foster home, the very last one I went to before I turned sixteen and aged out. I remember coming here, fearful, and meeting Louie, who hugged me. I hadn't been hugged in years, and it shocked me. It was still one of the happiest days of my life.

I go over to her side, stroking her greying

red hair and sighing. I'd do anything to be able to afford to wake her up. For Louie. For me.

I leave three quarters of my wages on the side, and Louie looks down at the money, right as his stomach grumbles. I smile and nod. "Should I go and get something for us?" he asks.

"And for the week. For you," I tell him, ruffling his hair.

"Thank you," he says quietly. "One day, I'm going to be an enforcer like you and pay you back for all these years. I'm going to protect you."

"You're my brother in every way that matters, and family don't owe each other debts like this," I gently tell him. "And with how smart you are, I hope to the goddess you become someone so much better than me."

"Impossible," he says with a grin.

"Be careful on the streets," I warn him as he picks up a few of the coins and shoves them into his faded brown trousers. I need to buy him some new clothes soon, judging from the tears and holes in his blue shirt. One thing I love about Louie is that he never complains, never asks for clothes or for anything that costs money except for food. I wish I could give him more, but I can't.

"The monsters can't catch me, I'm too fast," he exclaims before bolting out of the door.

I chuckle as I sit down in the chair by the side of her bed, picking up her pale hand. "He doesn't have a clue, does he, mom? But he looks so much like dad."

Silence and the gentle hum of the magic surrounding her is my only reply, and I can't even remember what her voice is like anymore. She was my foster mom for a few years, far longer than any of the other ten before her, and she always asked me to call her *mom*. "One day, I'm going to wake you up so you can see Louie growing into a strong man. I'm going to make sure he gets a good job and stays far away from the true dangers of this city."

I hope she can hear me. I hope it gives her some comfort to know I'm here, but a part of me wonders if she would resent me. I'm the reason she is like this. I'm the reason her mate is dead. I close my eyes and blow out a shaky breath. The monster hasn't come back, not for years, and I have no reason to suspect he will now. But if he does, this time, I won't be a helpless child, unable to stop him from murdering my foster parents. I don't know if he killed my biological parents, no one does, but he killed every enforcer family that took me in. I try not to think of it, of all the death that haunted me like he did. My monster, my lurking shadow. I stay with my foster mom for a little longer before cleaning up the house, doing the washing and tidying in her room before Louie gets back, and then we cook dinner together before eating.

"Can I come to yours to play a game of kings?" he asks, referring to the card game we play on quiet nights, especially weekends like today, as I wash up and he dries the plates.

"I'd usually have you over, but I'm meeting Nerelyth for drinks tonight. It's her birthday," I tell him softly. Most kids his age would prefer to play with their friends and have them over, but Louie has never been good at making friends. He keeps to himself.

"Okay," he replies, his voice tinged with sadness. Loneliness. He only has me and his mom, but she can't read him stories, play games and help with the complicated enchantment work he is learning at school. After grabbing my bag, I kiss the top of his head before I leave, closing the door behind me and resting my head back against it, my eyes drooping. I'm so tired and I could use a long nap, not a night of partying for Nerelyth's birthday.

I sigh and push myself off the wall before heading up to my apartment. It is partially paid for by the Enforcer Guild, one of the half decent things they do for their employees. The night sky glitters like a thousand moons as I get to my floor and look up at the sunroof far above. Three actual moons hang in the sky somewhere, but I can't see them from here, and I wish I could. They say looking at the three moons and making a wish is the only way for the dragon goddess to hear you. I'm sure it's not true, but I still look up sometimes and wish. I shove my key into the lock, wondering if I have any enchanted wine left over from last time Nerelyth came over, and push into my cold apartment. If I get dressed quickly, I might even have time to finish the extremely spicy romance book I was reading last night, on the way to the bar.

"Posy, where are you?" I shout out as I head

in. "I bought some of those meat strips you like from the market, as I'm going out tonight with Nerelyth. It's her birthday, remember?"

I've been mostly absent for the last two days and not had much time to spend with Posy—my roommate who happens to be a bat and stuck that way thanks to a witch's curse. I drop my bag on the side and look around in the darkness before sighing. Clicking my fingers, balls of warm white light within small glass spheres flood my apartment with light from where they are attached to the wall. I search around the main area, a small kitchen with two counters, a magical food storage box, and a large worn sofa pressed against the wall. It looks nearly the same as when I moved in, I notice, except for my two bookcases in the corridor leading to the bathroom and bedroom, full of romance books I've collected over the years. My prized possessions.

Escapism at its finest.

"Posy, come on. You can't still be mad at me?" I holler in frustration as I walk into the tiny bathroom, which is empty. "Bats are nocturnal, so I know you're awake and ignoring me, but I don't have time to chase you around this apartment all night."

I hear a small rustling noise from my bedroom, and I smile as I walk over and push the door open.

Clicking my fingers, two lights burn to life above my bed, and I go still. My heart nearly stops because it's not Posy in my bedroom.

There's a monster sitting on my bed.

CHAPTER TWO

Large wings.

Grey skin.

Muscular, massive shoulders and thick arms.

"Get the hell out!" I shout, a scream dying in my throat as I take a step away. I pull my dagger out from the clip on my thigh and hold it out between us as I quickly look for Posy, not seeing her anywhere. There's a friggin' monster in my room.

A wave of magic whips into my hand, the sting of it cold and piercing. My dagger flips across the room as I flinch, and it embeds itself in the wall with a thud. The monster doesn't even lift its head. He's... reading—my spicy romance book, of all things—as he sits on my bed. My double bed looks tiny with him sitting there, his dark hair soft and curling down his shoulders.

What the fuck?

My eyes widen as I look at this monster. He's a male. That much I'm sure of, and he's huge. He's sitting in the middle of my bed, reading my book from last night, looking like he's meant to be there. His skin is dark grey and almost velvety. Massive black wings stretch out of his back, but they're pulled in at his sides. Black horns curl out of the top of his thick black hair on his head, and if he wasn't a monster, I might even say he's handsome. He's shirtless, and he has pants on, but a tiny weird part of me focuses on the lack of a shirt for a second. No one looks that good shirtless—except this monster, it seems.

He is so big, and I'm sure he could snap me like a twig. Who the hell is he? What is he? More importantly—why is he in my bedroom?

"This is an interesting book for an innocent doe like you to be reading, Calliophe Maryann Sprite."

I freeze, my heart pounding as his deep,

sensual voice fills my room. How does he know my full name?

He looks up at me with hauntingly beautiful amethyst eyes and smirks. "Speechless, Doe?"

"Get the fuck out of my room!" I shout, grabbing the nearest thing on my side table and throwing it at him. He catches the stuffed purple teddy bear in his hand, then raises an eyebrow as his lips twitch with humor.

"Don't run," he purrs.

I glare as I grab the next thing, which is a cheap statue of the goddess, and I throw that straight at him instead. The statue crashes into his hand, smashes into pieces on impact, and he simply sighs in annoyance as he begins to stand. My old bed creaks as I grab my precious books from the corridor as I back away and throw them at him as I retreat. He catches them all like it's a game. I can't hear anything but my heartbeat, and I can't see anything but those wings that have haunted me for so many years. My monster had wings. It's all I can remember of him before he killed every parent I ever had.

Wings. The beat of wings fills my ears as I

burn with anger. My monster is back to kill me. I turn and run to the sofa, jumping on it as I pull out the two daggers I have hidden down on one side and crouch down in the corner. He casually strolls down the corridor, and he blocks the way to the only exit from my apartment as he faces me and crosses his arms. "Do you really believe that you, a tiny little mortal, will be able to stop me?"

"Come closer. Find out," I taunt. If he is going to kill me, I'm going down with a fight. I haven't survived monsters all these years, my entire life, to die easily at the hands of one.

He laughs, the sound deep and frightening. Arrogant son of a bitc—

I see a flash of black right before Posy flies straight into his face, clawing at him with her tiny, almost purple, bat wings. Posy is only a tiny bat and no more than the size of his hand as he grabs her by the scruff of her neck and holds her up in front of him. She still fights. The more I look at him, I realize he can't be the monster who hunted me. Those purple eyes aren't black, dark and cold like my monster's were. Still, those wings... my monster must be what he is. "What is this thing?" he asks.

I would laugh if he wasn't trying to kill me. Posy yells, "Die, die, die. You supernatural monster! This is my home, and I don't care how horny my roommate is. She is not fucking a monster when I'm living here!"

By the old gods. My cheeks burn.

The monster smirks and looks over at me. "You have a talking bat."

"Let her go!" I demand as I look between them and the door. I don't know how I will make it to the door to run if I go for Posy.

He sighs, and Posy is still ranting away, unaware that no one is listening to her anymore. Or the fact this monster isn't my date and that he is here to kill me. "No. We are leaving."

"We are not," I say at the same time Posy declares, "Finally. Go to the monster's place and do the dirty. Between keeping me here as your pet and your new fuck buddy, I think you have a weird thing for bats."

"We bats can be very fun," the monster agrees with a hint of dry amusement that makes him seem almost mortal. Almost. He is very much not.

He lets Posy go, and she flies into my

bedroom, slamming the door shut. I need a better roommate/pet. Posy sucks.

"Then go and have fun somewhere else, or I'm going to pin those nice wings of yours to my wall," I say, holding the daggers up higher. Why he hasn't used his magic to rid me of them yet floats into the back of my mind. Maybe he is playing with me. "What are you, anyway?"

"Wyern," he coolly answers. "Haven't you seen any in your career?"

No, I haven't, or I'd be very dead. My blood runs cold as I take him in, a Wyern male, in my living room. The Wyerns are immortal, deadly, and everyone knows they are forbidden from entering Ethereal City. Some say they are fae—an old race of them. Some say they were created by the fae and are born monsters.

I should have known he's not a monster. Not exactly, but not far from one. From what I know, the Wyerns live in the Forgotten Lands, a punishment from my queen for the war they started thousands of years ago. Some say the sirens siding with the Fae Queen was the only way we won.

One trained Wyern male can slaughter ten trained fae in minutes.

My heart races as I take all of this in. If I call for help and they find me here with him, even if he is trying to kill me or take me somewhere, the queen will execute me for treason. "If the queen finds you here, which she will, we are both dead. Leave."

He steps towards me, an amused smirk on his lips. "Your precious queen would be very honored if I turned up in her city, but perhaps a little angry I came for you and not to see her."

"What?"

He glowers at me. "Are you mortals truly this dense? We. Are. Leaving."

"We certainly are not going anywhere!"

He takes another step forward, and I start to back away until the back of my knees touch the sofa.

I lash out at him with my daggers, cutting through his arm, and it bubbles with blood. He doesn't even notice as he grabs my hands, squeezing tight enough I'm forced to drop the daggers with a yelp. I kick at his shin, which is like a rock and only hurts me, and he grabs me by the waist and throws me over his shoulder like I weigh nothing. I scream and kick him in the stomach and slam my hands on his solid back, but nothing makes his arm shift from his iron tight grip on me.

Magic wraps around me firmly, its icy sting burning into my skin, and I hiss in pain as my head spins. I hate magic.

"Let me go!" I scream over and over. He only laughs like it's deeply amusing to him as he walks out of my apartment by kicking my front door open. I look up in horror as he spreads his massive wings out, and magic lashes around us as he shoots up the flights of stairs. The stairs whip up around us as I scream, ducking my head as my stomach feels like a million butterflies have burst to life. He crashes through the glass, bits of it cutting into my arms, and launches us into the night sky above the city. His wings beat near my face, and I stop trying to fight him. If he drops me, I'm dead.

It doesn't stop the lash of magic that slams into my head and knocks me out cold seconds later, leaving me dreaming of wings and star-filled night skies.

CHAPTER
THREE

"*Take her, Vivienne. Just take her and run!*"

I snuggle down into my bed, clutching the sheets tighter as I hear crashing noises, shouting and doors slamming. It's happening again. He has come for me again. No, no, no...

"*We both can run and fight him,*" *my foster mom pleads. I've only been here a year. It's too soon for the monster to come for me.*

"*No. She needs someone to live for her,*" *my foster dad exclaims, and the door to my room slams.* "*She is just six years old, and all she has known is death. Someone has to tell her why, someone has to explain the truth.*"

"He'll never stop," Vivienne cries. *"We shouldn't have taken her in after—"*

"I have no regrets. We do this for the Guild. For our queen and what she gave," he interrupts her. Hands pull my quilt back, and I look up at my foster dad with panicked eyes. His voice is gentle and as soft as his brown eyes as he stares down at me. "You need to go with Vivienne and run. It's here, and I'm going to stop it."

"But—"

He hushes me, kissing my forehead. "It's been an honor to care for you, Calliophe Maryann Sprite. Live."

I gulp, tears falling down my cheeks as Vivienne picks me up, holding me to her. She always picks me up, telling me how small I am for my age, and I cling to her neck, wishing this is all a dream. It's not real. The monster isn't real.

I hide my head in her bright red hair, peeping out to look at my foster dad standing by the door. He looks over his shoulder, holding a silver sword in front of him, an enchanted rope dangling from his fingers. "Live for all of us, Calliophe."

Vivienne and he share a look for a moment before she carries me to the window, and my foster dad opens the door, shutting it behind us. Vivienne opens the window before sitting on the edge, the icy wind blowing around us, snowflakes littering the air. My breath comes out like smoke as I shiver. "Hold on to me and don't let go."

I nod against her shoulder as she jumps off the window ledge into the snowy night, and I cling to her as she lands in a thump on the ground. Vivienne wraps her arms around me before she sprints across the grass, leaping over the small brown fence and past the swing tied to the old oak tree. I keep looking over her shoulder for the monster inside my home, but no lights are on, and there is nothing but the glittering night sky until I hear a male scream.

Vivienne stops and slowly turns back, holding me tightly to her. She puts me down on the ground and points at the woods a few feet away. "I have to go back for him. I love him. You have to run. Don't stop running. Find someone, anyone, and tell them to call the Guild. Tell them we're in trouble, but you need to run."

"I don't want to be on my own," I wail as she lowers me to the ground, pulling my arms from her and stepping back.

She kisses my forehead. "I'm so sorry, but he is all I have."

"You have me."

I try to catch her hand, but she pushes me away before she runs back to the house. Tears fall down my cheeks, and I shake from head to toe as I turn and run into the tall, dark trees. I cling to the nearest tree, the bark scratching my hands and the branches snatching in my hair. Everything is silent for a moment before I hear Vivienne scream and cry out, and then there is silence once more. I hear a door being smashed open, and I turn to see a male stepping out into the shadows. He has gigantic wings that spread out like shadows in the night, but I can't see anything else as he turns my way.

Terrified, I run deep into the forest, letting it swallow me in its darkness.

I wake up with my heart racing fast in my chest as I blink and look around, tasting the icy sting of magic on my tongue. It was just a dream. I click my fingers, and lights burn up in the room, and I go still.

It wasn't a dream.

I've been kidnapped by that arrogant, and a little beautiful, monster. The bat guy. Shit. I take in the scents around me on the soft sheets, and I frown. Masculine. This is that monster's bedroom. By the goddess. I push the dark midnight blue sheets off me, noticing my boots are missing as I look at the bedroom. Expensive and exotic wood makes the massive bed I'm on, and there are matching wardrobes and a dresser. They go well with the dark red walls and polished oak beams that run across the ceiling and the carmine curtains. I look back at the headboard, which is one magnificent piece of wood carved and polished.

My legs are shaky from the magic and a little fear as I walk across the hardwood floors and to the window. The window is massive, ceiling to floor, with black squares all over it. My heart stops as I look outside at the unfamiliar mountains.

We aren't in Ethereal City.

If I had to guess where I am... The Wyern are said to live in the Forgotten City, in the thick mountains to the north of Ethereal City. I've only ever seen these mountains from a far distance, and then they were nothing more than a dot on the horizon. Now, I'm in the middle of them. The mountains are steep, covered in jagged spikes and snow. It's kind of pretty, with the night sky hanging behind, the sun slowly rising.

I think it's safe to bet I'm not going to work today.

My heart is still racing, and I will myself to calm down. If the Wyern wanted me dead, I would be dead. No, he must want me for something else, and that gives me time to make a plan and escape.

Somehow.

I glance around to see if I can find anything useful to defend myself, but there isn't much, just a dresser, two wardrobes, and a rug. I search the wardrobe and drawers, finding male clothes and nothing else. Unless I plan to throw socks at him, my search isn't going well. I find my boots by the end of the bed and slide them on, finding the two small knives I hid in the heel have been taken. My mouth feels dry as I go to the dark wooden double doors and test the silver handles to see if I'm locked in. The doors click open to my surprise, and I peek out into the corridor. The same dark wood floor stretches down a long and wide passageway, and there's a dark red, patterned runner running down the entire length of it. There are endless doors on either side and more light orbs lighting up the space on the ceiling. I hear vague scuffling, voices and music from the left side, and the right is completely empty and silent but a dead end by the looks of it.

I quietly shut the door behind me as I step out and head down the passageway, wishing I had some of my weapons on me. I try a few handles on my way, but all of them are locked, to my annoyance.

I blow out a shaky breath when I see a door open a few feet away, the noise coming from in there and orange light shining out the gap. My hair falls around my shoulders, and I tuck a strand behind my ear as I follow the sounds of the music. It's old music, but it's sensual and soft and not what I expect to hear. I walk the final steps to the door and peek into the massive room. Pillars and tapestries line the walls, all of it old and stunning, and the soft music is being played by magic throughout the air, the taste of it coating my tongue. Several cushioned areas lie around three giant waterfalls with statues of the goddess in the center of them, water pouring out of her hands. The room is warm and cozy, but maybe not the people inside it. Wyerns. Each one of them looks slightly different, all dark or grey skinned, and there are at least twenty female mortals in here with them. By the moans, they're clearly having fun, and I try not to look too long at any one of them. They are all having sex.

Except a few. Like the male on the seating area nearest me. He is different from the others; his light grey skin is littered with small and large scars, and his horns have been cut off. He doesn't have wings, and his eyes are a soft forest green as he looks my way. He has a grey shirt on that a female with long brown hair is pawing at. In fact, he has three females lying on his lap, and one of them is stroking him underneath his trousers. He still watches me, tilting his head to the side with a little smirk on his lips as one of the other females runs her hand through his short brown hair. Dear god, I just walked into a monster orgy. Absolutely brilliant. I really hope that is not what they brought me here for. I haven't had sex with anyone for over two years thanks to my work. And even then, I prefer a heated few hours at their place and then I disappear. I don't do long-term anything.

I'm certainly not staying here if this is the plan.

"The doe is awake," the male shouts, and many male laughs follow. Fuck it.

I push the door open and head inside, letting the door slam against the wall. "Kidnapping is illegal. I'm leaving if one of you will be kind enough to show me the door."

"I don't think so, little doe," the male says, gently pushing the females off him and standing. He walks up to me, towering over me. "We've been waiting for you to wake up. Do you want a drink?"

I glower at him. "No."

"Come on, relax. Have you never seen a royal court having fun before?"

"This is a royal court?" I say dryly. "Looks more like—"

"Ah, be nice. You don't insult someone's home when you're a guest," he interrupts.

"I'm not a guest. I didn't come here willingly!" I protest.

"Still, be nice, little mortal."

He pats me on the head and looks back at

the beautiful females on the sofa, who giggle. By the goddess. It stinks of sex in here, and the moans are getting louder than the music. "No."

"How about that drink?"

"No," I repeat, and he smiles at me. "I want to know why I'm here? Where's the male that kidnapped me and took me?"

He sighs, stepping closer, and offers me his hand. He smells of wine and bad decisions. Nerelyth would love him. "My name is Lorenzo Eveningstar."

I don't take it, considering what he has just been doing, and raise an eyebrow. He chuckles deep and low. "Usually when someone tells you their name, you shake their hand and tell them your name. Do mortals like yourself no longer know manners?"

"So you don't know my name? After kidnapping me—"

"I didn't kidnap you," he quickly corrects me.

I rub my forehead. "My name is Calliophe."

"Ah, I did wonder if it was Doe," he smiles and looks me over. "I don't know what my king is thinking."

King?

The Wyern King kidnapped me?

By the goddess, I'm dead. I'm so dead.

I cross my arms with bravado I don't have. "Why am I here, Lorenzo?"

"I believe that is for King Emerson Eveningstar to answer," another voice answers.

I turn to look over at the female walking towards me. She's fae. This female is a full-blooded fae. She's wearing pretty much nothing but a slip of silver sheer fabric that makes up a dress that is wrapped around her large breasts and thin waist before falling to her feet. She is flawless. Fae always are. Everything about them is designed to trick mortals like myself into trusting them. Her beautiful silvery blonde hair that is loosely held up, curls and falls around her shoulders and slender face. She stops in front of me, and her eyes light up in different shades of purple and blue.

Lorenzo smiles at the fae female. "Calliophe, meet another member of our court, Zurine Quarzlin. Rine, she is looking for Emerson."

Zurine looks me over from the top of my head to my feet, focusing on my eyes for a second. I search her eyes and see nothing but sadness hidden within them. "Why don't I show you the way?"

My smile is tight. "Alright."

She waves her hand at the door, and I follow her through, glancing back to see Lorenzo swaggering back to the females. "I imagine you're confused and worried, but ignore the males here. As usual, they think with their cocks and not their minds half the time, much like the rest of our court. That's not why he brought you here. The mortal females come to our court willingly for the pleasure."

I dryly chuckle. "Confused? I was kidnapped by a monster."

"My king isn't a monster," she says softly, her voice full of affection. "Even if he appears as one."

"I hadn't seen a Wyern before, so to me, he looked like one. Then he kidnapped me...," I drawl.

She laughs lightly as we head down the corridor, and our conversation drifts off until I need to fill the silence instead of feeling so nervous. "I haven't seen many fae before. Only one or two. Most don't come down to the lower parts of Ethereal City, and my work doesn't lead me anywhere near the castle or the fae district."

She doesn't look down at me. "Then you are lucky, mortal."

"Perhaps," I mutter. "So you're part of this court even when you're not one of them?"

She looks at me this time as we go through a door and into a corridor with long windows on each side. "Yes, and for what it is worth, you can trust me. You won't be able to trust many here."

One of these Wyerns is my monster, hunted me from birth, and I won't trust anyone here until I find who it is. And kill them.

"For what it's worth, I don't believe trusting anyone here is going to end with anything but my death."

She smiles at that. "You're a smart mortal."

Weird compliment.

"Although you're not all mortal, are you? You definitely have a bit of fae in your bloodline with those eyes. Who was it?"

I look at the shiny floor. "I don't know any of my family."

"Oh, I'm sorry. Is your hair natural or enchanted?"

"Enchanted by a dodgy spell, and I haven't been able to change it back since I was fifteen," I explain with a chuckle. "It was a lesson in why you don't buy enchantments from strangers on the market."

She laughs. "I think pink is your color."

I smile for a moment at the fae female. "Thank you."

She leads me down several corridors, through a few more empty rooms, each more confusing than the last until I'm thoroughly lost. We both stay silent until we come to a massive pair of imposing doors at the end of a corridor. These are curved to almost look like bat wings, and they are old, much like the walls around it. Zurine pulls the doors open and moves to the side. "I'll leave you to him. Remember, with these males, they will bite if you push too much."

She lowers her voice. "But most of them have a soft heart underneath it all. Especially the king."

I walk into the gigantic room, eyeing the red carpet that runs up to a platform at the back of the room, where a king sits on a massive throne. The throne is made of black oak, with five long spikes making the headboard that looks like the spiked mountains outside. The throne room, which I'm guessing this is, is magnificent. Pillars line the walls with windows between them, lined with black squares. Fae light, a rare and expensive form of magic, hovers in tiny little stars across the entire ceiling, and it makes it look like the endless night sky.

Beautiful and daunting.

I turn my gaze to the throne, pulled towards it with an invisible tug deep in my chest.

The king sits on his throne, his legs spread wide, his wings hanging off the sides of the seat. Tight black leathers spread across his chest and down his arms, and into his leather trousers. The shine of the leather reminds me that they must be enchanted, maybe by himself. I'm not sure what powers the Wyerns have, but if they can effortlessly fight the fae, making enchantments should be nothing. His hand is dug into the brown hair of a female between his knees, her head resting on his knee. The room smells of sex, and looking at the pair of them, it's clear what they have been doing. The female doesn't even look at me as she stares up at Emerson, and he tilts his head to the side as his eyes lock on mine. The move is pure predator-like with a stillness only an immortal can have. "What do you want?"

I shiver from his deep, cold voice, but I don't cower. "That's the very question I came to ask you. Considering you kidnapped me."

He stands up off his throne with fury in his eyes, leaving the female on her knees, and walks towards me with a casualness that makes me fear him. He is so tall I have to arch my neck to look at him as he stops close. "Mortals bow to kings. Get on your knees."

"No," I bite out.

A lash of magic slams into my knees, and I fall to my knees before the king, unwillingly, and I glare at him as his magic surrounds me, holding me in place.

He looks down at me like I'm a bug to a bird flying high above. To him, I might as well be. "Next time I tell you to bow, you bow. Next time I tell you anything, you do it. Welcome to my court, Doe. Stay here."

He walks past me, leaving me locked in his magic as the mortal female rushes past me to follow him out. Only when the throne room doors slam shut behind me does the magic fade away, and I bite back the urge to scream.

I really, really hate the king.

CHAPTER FOUR

I slam my fists repeatedly against the throne room doors in frustration. "Let me out! Let me out!"

The doors don't budge, neither do the handles, which feel like ice to touch. Magic.

I scream in frustration, but no one comes for me, and I swear I hear a male laugh on the other side of the door. Eventually, I give up when my hands start to hurt, and back away from the door.

Wrapping my arms around myself, I look around the room before walking over to the windows. Wherever this is inside the castle, it's definitely at the highest point or near it. The mountain spikes look lower, and I know if

I jumped out this window somehow, I'd impale myself on one of them. Birds duck and dive through the air on the breeze, dancing to an invisible element, and I watch them for a long time until they disappear into the black mountains.

The sun is shining high in the sky, climbing with every hour that passes as I stay locked in here. My stomach is rumbling and my mouth is dry when the doors finally open, and I climb up off the floor. I cautiously watch as Lorenzo walks in, followed by four Wolven males. I recognize some of them from the first room I saw, but now they have clothes on at least. Lorenzo flashes me a toothy smile, and I glare at him as Zurine wanders in after them. She walks my way, smiling softly at me.

I cross my arms. "He locked me in here."

"He's not in the best of moods today," she tells me gently with amusement in her eyes. "Seems you've riled him up."

"It wasn't me. It looked like he was in a foul mood well before he kidnapped me and locked me in here."

"You will understand why you're here in a moment. We're about to have a court meeting, and you're invited as a guest," she kindly tells me, waving in the direction the others went. "Please, come and sit with me."

I do not have a choice, and we both know it. I reluctantly follow her behind the throne room where there is a large circular slate table and brown leather, backless stools spread around it. Lorenzo and the others are talking quietly by the side of the table, and they go silent when we get close.

Zurine takes a seat, and I sit down next to her, crossing my legs and resting my hands on them to stop them from shaking. Lorenzo comes and sits next to me, close enough his arm brushes my arm, and I move away.

The four other Wyerns take some of the remaining seats while we wait for the king, and I feel them all staring at me as I keep my eyes straight ahead.

"Let me do some introductions. Everyone, this is Calliophe Maryann Sprite. She's a mortal who works at Monster Activities Division of the Enforcer Guild and is considered one of the best they have," Lorenzo states.

I turn to look at him. "Someone's been doing their homework."

"Only when young, beautiful mortals are the research topic," he replies with a flirty tone.

"Charming, but don't waste your flirting skills on me. I'm sure there are other poor mortals for you to bless," I coolly reply, because he is charming, and good looking, but he is one of them. I've never been good at flirting, and as Nerelyth tells me, I don't need to flirt when I'm pretty and want nothing long-term with anyone. Long-term means there is a risk of my monster coming and killing them. I can't have the happy ending, the family and one true love. I've been on four dates, had three lovers, and that has been enough. Still, I can see why willing mortals wish to come here and be with them. The Wyerns remind me of the male fae: beautiful, alluring, and likely much better in bed than mortal males.

One of the other Wyerns chuckles low. "She has you sussed, Lorz."

This one is shorter than the others as I turn to face him. His wings are near pitch black and tall, and his skin is a similar tone. His eyes are like melted honey as he looks over at me and warmly smiles. His head is completely shaven, and three silver earrings are clipped to the tip of his left ear. "I'm Felix Masterlight. This is my brother, Nathiel. It's a pleasure."

His voice is like honey, too. His brother looks nearly identical. So much so, I would say they might be twins. Nathiel doesn't smile at me, but he simply inclines his head.

I nod mine back. "I would say it's nice to meet you, but..."

One of the Wyerns on the other side of the table coolly chuckles. "You've been kidnapped and dragged here, and you believe we are monsters."

I look over at the male who spoke, his voice gruff and playful, and the fourth court member. These Wyerns look like the opposite of each other. The one who spoke has dirty blond hair that hasn't been brushed and falls down to his ears, and he has more of a slim build. The male next to him has jet black hair, is more muscular than even the king, and his face is littered with small scars. He scowls at me, and it doesn't faze me like it would do most people. I face monsters every day.

"You're right, Ferris. I don't believe she likes us," the scowling one says.

The blond runs his eyes over me. "I'm sure I could find a way to encourage her to like us."

"Mortals are a waste of everyone's time unless they are on their knees. Begging," the other male coolly states to his brother, not even bothering to look at me.

Ferris laughs low. "True, Julian. True."

Bastards.

We sit in silence for a while, the silence getting more and more daunting, until I hear the doors slam open and his footsteps echo across the floor. He storms into the throne room, and I twist my neck to watch as he walks in, past me and around the table, before taking a seat.

Everyone bows their head once, and he looks directly across at me when I don't bow mine.

He may have forced me to my knees, but I won't willingly ever bow to him.

I look away first, needing to or it's hard to breathe, and find Zurine carefully watching me.

"We're going to make it simple for you to understand," King Emerson begins, his tone bored. "I brought you here—"

"Kidnapped," I correct.

"Don't interrupt the king," Julian growls at me, making the hair on my arms spike up.

"We brought you here," King Emerson continues, no amount of sarcasm missing from his words, "because you've been hunting hybrids and capturing them."

I furrow my brow. "The hybrids? That's why I'm here?"

"Yes," Lorenzo takes over. "Our information states you've caught three of them without dying."

I nod. "Do you know where they're from?"

"No. We want to hire you to find out where the hybrids are from, to hunt them privately for us. You can work alongside your division if you wish, but this would be a private matter for you and not to be discussed with anyone," Lorenzo explains.

I look at the king, who is sitting with his arms crossed, watching me with the same bored expression he had when he got in here. He kidnapped me to ask for my help. I almost laugh. "Why would I do that? I don't want to help you and end up killed by the Fae Queen.

She would kill me for even considering helping you."

The king tilts his head to the side. "You have a ward, do you not?"

"Yes," I bite out.

Zurine places her hand on my arm, and I nearly jump. "What my king suggests is that the young boy who you look after and his mother in the medical sleep might do well if you took our job. It is a job, not a favor, and you will be heavily paid."

King Emerson slides his eyes to me. "Find out who did this and find the hybrids' leader, and we will pay you an exorbitant amount. So much coin that you can move out of that hovel you live in and buy somewhere nice to live out your mortal life. Do we have a deal?"

I feel like King Emerson might not have heard this word often in his life, but here goes... "No."

His eyes narrow into sharp blades. "You would let your ward and his mother suffer? You would let the hybrids continue to rip apart your fellow mortals, out of what? Pride?"

I glare right back as I stand up and place my hands on the table. "I would do anything for Louie and my foster mom, but helping you will end up getting me killed. I'm not stupid. It's why you're asking me in the first place. Because you can't search in Ethereal City. The Fae Queen—"

He frowns and cuts me off midsentence. "You're a coward, Calliophe Sprite. How disappointing."

"Calliophe, we will protect you from the queen and her spies in the city," Zurine softy warns as I sit down . "Yes, there is a risk, and it is your choice. We are not here to force you into helping us."

Lorenzo looks at the king, and some kind of silent message seems to spread between them before he speaks. "You will receive ten percent of the million coins we will pay you. You will get the other ninety percent when you find out who they are. If you're not dead, that is."

A million coins. By the goddess. With that sort of money, I could wake my foster mom and take them both to live happily in Junepit City for the rest of our lives. I wouldn't have to wake up at the crack of dawn every day, fight and risk my life for scraps of coins to get us by. I could live and choose a real future for myself that isn't just a life I have to live to survive. All of it lies right in front of me, as risky as it is. Also, this is the closest I have ever gotten to finding out who the monster is that hunted me as a child and killed everyone I ever loved back then.

"But if I die," I say, leaning forward, "it's all for nothing, and my ward is left alone. I have too much to lose. Find someone else."

"I knew the mortal would be too selfish to do this," Julian sneers. "If we—"

King Emerson cuts him off. "We are not discussing that option again, Julian. Your anger with mortals clouds your judgment."

I rub my forehead. "Why do you want to know who is making the hybrids? How does it affect you?"

King Emerson barely even glances at me as Lorenzo answers. "We want to know because they took one of our people. Our sister, the princess of our race. She was taken three days ago, and we can't find her."

I look between King Emerson and Lorenzo... who never mentioned he is a prince. "Our sister?"

Emerson's eyes are like icy frost blowing

over my skin with pepper sweet kisses. "Is there a problem?"

I'm in too deep because I'm actually considering this. Nerelyth is going to drown me in the seas when she hears about all of this. "How old is your sister? Why would they take her? How was she taken exactly?"

King Emerson looks like he has won, and I hate it. "She's young, nearly your age, and inexperienced in combat. They came, and they took her when we were away. Those left killed at least twenty of the hybrids, but there were endless amounts of them. They knew how to get in, where to find her, and how to get her out without alerting many."

I point out the obvious. "Someone fed them information, then?"

"My people are bound to me and cannot betray the royal blood. Whoever it is must have walked these halls at some time. Perhaps when my father or grandfather ruled the Forgotten City," he informs me.

Lorenzo's chair groans as he moves. "We want her back alive and will pay you. What have you to lose?"

I hate that he has a point in a way, but this

is a risk. I'll be working with monsters to hunt down a bigger monster.

I sigh. "Why bother kidnapping me and not just asking me nicely back at my home?"

Emerson doesn't look remotely sorry. "Because you'll be staying here. It's safer for you while you are under our protection and working for us."

"I really don't think so. If you want me to work on this case, I'll need to be in Ethereal City, not here in the mountains. Plus, people are going to realize I'm missing, and that's going to draw attention," I counter. "I will take this job, but the condition is that I stay in my apartment."

He throws his own condition right back at me. "For the week. The weekends you spend here."

"Fine." I grit my teeth. The weekends, I can spend investigating the Wyerns and who might want to hunt down me.

He crosses his thick arms. "There was never an option. You work for me or you die."

"You're not my king," I remind him. "But I'm no coward, and I will find your sister. I want to stop whoever is creating the hybrids just as much as you. They are killing innocent mortals and supernaturals. This is my work, and you're right, I'm damn good at it."

His lips tilt up. "Still a coward under all that pretty pink hair. Pretending to be brave won't stop that fear in your chest from crawling itself out."

"Says the heartless monster king on a cold throne, hidden in a corner of the world, asking a mortal to help him because no one else would dare."

The room goes deadly silent.

Shit. Maybe I shouldn't have said that. I don't have it in me to apologize, but there is a little fear that crawls up my throat with how Emerson's eyes narrow on me. He looks at Lorenzo. "Have her trailed in the day, and one of us sleeps at hers at night. She is not to be left alone."

I want to argue I can look after myself, but the truth is, if the hybrids are working in groups, I'll take whatever protection I can get.

They can take the bumpy sofa and deal with my psychotic bat roommate.

She loves guests. Not.

Lorenzo nods sharply. "I'll arrange it all, brother."

"Everyone leave. Except you, Doe."

My eyes widen as they all stand and leave, and I don't even try to stand up. Lorenzo pats my back once before leaving. I assume it's some sort of good luck pat. I keep my eyes on the king, my hands gripping the seat of the chair tightly as he stands up and walks around the table. When the throne room doors are shut, he pushes the chair to my right aside and sits on the edge of the table next to me, his wing brushing so close it could touch my hand.

I lift my head. "What else do you want?"

He leans down, leaving our faces inches apart. This close, I can only smell how good his scent is and see how the leathers are tight across his body, his face smooth and sculpted into perfection. He is a beautiful monster indeed. "If you're caught by any fae, you do not mention my name. You do not tell a single fae a word of this, or I'll kill you myself. Do you understand?"

"Threats are idle. If a fae knew of this, I'd be dead way before you'd get to me."

And I'd be thankful for it, I bet.

His eyes seem to swirl like rippling water. Still shallow water that you'd walk into, unaware of the current underneath waiting to snatch you up. "Watch your back, mortal. Make one wrong step, and death will seem like a mercy."

My heart is racing fast as he leans back and then pushes off the table before walking away. Only when he is gone do I remember to breathe.

CHAPTER FIVE

"That went well, I trust."

I turn to face Lorenzo as I step out of the throne room, happy to escape that place after being stuck in there all day. He is waiting out in the corridor for me, his arms crossed as he leans against the wall. "Is he always like that?"

Lorenzo sighs and straightens. He may not look much like his brother, but he holds himself in a similar way, and now that I know, I can see some shared features. "Yes. I'm the fun brother, and Emerson is... well, he was brought up to be king. You don't stay king of the Wyerns without being ruthless."

I don't know what to say to that, and

thankfully, Lorenzo changes the subject. "Ready to go back to Ethereal City?"

I nod with a shiver. "Yes, but I don't look forward to flying back."

"Flying is the dramatic way to travel that far," Lorenzo tells me with a secretive curve of his lips. "The mirrors take about five hours to travel through, but it feels like minutes for us. So you'll be home just before the sun sets, I bet."

"Mirrors?" I ask with a frown.

He ignores me and walks away, and I'm left with no choice but to follow after him. "As I'm sleeping over, does that mean I get invited into your bed?"

I nearly choke on thin air. "Absolutely not."

"Damn. We're not allowed to touch you, but I've always been interested in forbidden things," he says.

"Forbidden by who?"

He pushes a door open, and I step into another corridor. By the goddess, this place is a maze. "Emerson. The moody git doesn't want anyone touching you and distracting you from your job. A waste, as our sleepovers could be so much more interesting and fun."

"I'm not interested, Lorenzo," I bluntly tell him.

He pretends to stab himself in the chest. "How will I survive now?"

I roll my eyes at his dramatics, even as I smile. This monster is funny at least, and I can rule him out of my list of who is my monster. He doesn't have wings. I wonder why for a moment, before he opens a door to a small room full of glowing mirrors. Mirrors fill every wall, each one of them encased in a gold frame. The floors are shiny, reflecting my image like the mirrors, and it's very warm in here, which is strange, as magic always feels like ice. There is magic in the air, strange and different from what I felt before, and Lorenzo closes the door behind us. "Welcome to the Speculis. One of our greatest secrets."

"Is this how you get the mortals I saw here?"

"Yes, and fae, sirens, and especially the Snake females. They are great with their tongu—"

"I don't need to know that," I cut him off.

He grins. "Fine, but yes. We always keep them blindfolded and wipe their memories before they go back. Before you ask, they always are aware of what they are agreeing to when coming here. Most beg."

Goose bumps litter my skin. "What do your females say?"

"Considering there are three female Wyerns left—they are very rare—not much. They have their own males for fun."

"Three? That's it?" I whisper.

"Shit. Don't repeat that," he says, rubbing his face. "Solandis being taken is messing with my head."

"Your sister was named after the dragon goddess?" I quietly ask, feeling his sorrow like it's my own for a moment. If Louie were taken, I'd do anything to get him back.

He waves his hand across the mirror and offers me his other hand. "Yes. She was born on Nocturno."

The Falling Night.

"So was I."

He looks right at me as I take his hand and frowns. "How unusual. Solandis would like you."

I don't know why I shared that. It's one of the only things I know about myself, from my limited records. Nocturno is the middle point of the year, a special day because the sun never rises in the sky and it's an eternal night. The old fairy tale used to explain this annual occurrence is that Nocturno was the day the dragon goddess died, and when her spirit left this world, the sun grieved and did not appear. Instead, the night sky burned with a million stars and the moons shone brighter than ever.

He takes a step towards the mirror, and I tighten my grip on his hand, which is soft. "Don't let go."

I barely get a second to brace myself as Lorenzo tugs me straight into the mirror, and we fall through it like it's thick water. I can't breathe, the warm magic suffocating me, and I start to panic even as Lorenzo's hand tightly pulls me along. Whatever this magic is, it's old and horrible, painting itself against my skin.

Suddenly, the magic disappears, and I gasp for air as we both stumble out into the street outside my apartment building. I look behind me at the wall, which is shimmering with gold magic right before it slowly fades away into nothing but stone.

"That was incredibly horrible."

"The first time is always the worst," he says with a teasing grin.

I chuckle and pull my hand away.

He smiles. "Oh, I thought we'd hold hands forever."

"I'm sure you can find another, more willing mortal to hold your hand," I dryly reply.

He winks at me. "Usually I like them to hold other things of mine."

I walked right into that one. I shake my head as I walk away and head into my apartment, noticing Lorenzo is right, and it's already night out. He strolls in after me, and I glance around, noticing a few people on the streets. Thankfully, none of them pay much attention as we head inside and up the stairs.

Lorenzo hands me keys halfway up. "Thanks. My weapons?"

"Emerson has them," he replies with a shrug.

I sigh. "You need to be careful while you're here in the city. Any supernatural is going to know what you are."

"They won't see me. I can fade away into shadows, and I'm damn good at it. It's why I'm here with you," he replies, taking the steps two at a time and getting ahead of me. Show off. "It's a royal gift."

"So not all Wyerns can do it?" I ask. I'm surprised it's so quiet in the building, and we are lucky we haven't passed anyone on the way up.

"No, but some of the powerful can use magic to hide themselves for a time."

I nod, all of a sudden feeling very tired, and the day is catching up to me. I keep quiet as I climb the rest of the stairs, glancing at Louie's floor as we pass it by. He won't find it suspicious. I haven't seen him today. He'll just think I'm out hunting monsters again... but the boss won't think the same thing. He is going to kill me. I'll just have to make it up that I was sick or something. Nerelyth can help me come up with something. We are good at covering each other's back. She's definitely going to notice that I didn't turn up for her birthday though, and I'm sure she is worried. Stress starts building into a headache as I get to my apartment door and unlock it. I head inside, clicking my fingers to turn the lights on as Lorenzo shuts the door behind us.

"So, where is my room?"

"Prince Lorenzo, here is your luxury bed," I sarcastically say, waving at the sofa. "I do hope it meets your high standards."

He laughs deeply behind me as I open my cupboards to find a snack, disappointingly finding them empty. Oh well, it's not the first time I haven't eaten for a whole day.

Posy flies in the room, hooking her claws onto the top of the counter and hanging upside down as she inspects us. "Of course you brought the bat back with you."

"Technically, you're more a bat than I," Lorenzo smoothly says and looks at me. "As children, we used to chase bats like this for sport. Why do you keep it here?"

"She's a mortal cursed to be a bat forever," I explain with a sigh. "Because of her sassy attitude, I bet."

I don't actually know why Posy was cursed, or by who. I found her injured and alone years ago, and I felt sorry for her. It's been something I've grown to regret over the years. I hoped she would turn back and the curse would end. It didn't.

Posy's sweet, innocent little eyes look at

me and, sometimes, when she doesn't speak, she looks very cute. Other times when she does speak, I'm tempted to throw her out of the window.

"This is Lorenzo, Posy. He'll be staying here tonight. In fact, we'll have more guests over than usual at night. It's part of a new job that I've taken."

"No," Posy snarkily replies.

I cross my arms. "You don't have a choice."

"I'm your roommate, and I don't agree to your bat fuck buddies moving in here."

"It's not exactly like you actually pay for anything! Remember, I pay for your food, this place and everything else. Try being grateful for once. Did you even notice I was kidnapped?"

She rolls her eyes. "Kidnapped? Sure. You're very overdramatic."

"Posy," I sigh in annoyance. "I just—"

She interrupts me. "The monster bat clearly didn't satisfy you. Is this why you have a new lover? He might not have wings, but he smells like a bat; still your thing, it seems. If you come back in this lovely, bitchy mood of yours after he is done, then there is no fixing you."

I shake my head. I'm too tired to deal with her tonight. Lorenzo is trying not to chuckle and failing.

"I like you, bat mortal," he exclaims as he strolls to the sofa, and it actually collapses under the weight of him because it's such a crappy sofa.

"Help yourself to whatever food you can find, which won't be a lot," I tell him as I walk past. "I'm going to sleep. Night."

"Good night, Calliophe."

Shutting the door behind me, I walk over to my bed and sit down on it, just where Emerson sat before, and his scent is still lingering in here. It reminds me he had my romance book, and as I look over at my side unit, I realize it's missing. He took it. Dammit. I was only halfway through it, and it was getting to the good part. After stripping my clothes and throwing them in the sink, I use enchanted soap to instantly clean my clothes before I hang them up to dry.

After having a shower, I get back into my worn purple pajama top and shorts before climbing into bed. As soon as my head hits the pillow, I fall asleep. Morning light trickles in through the window, waking me, and I sit up wondering if it's all a dream as I smell bacon. We don't have money for bacon. I walk out of my bedroom, rubbing my eyes as my stomach rumbles loudly. I'm surprised to see a very shirtless Lorenzo in my kitchen… cooking.

"I hope you like bacon, eggs, and pancakes. I got everything from the market this morning. You were right. Your ice storage and cupboards have shitloads of nothing in them. No wonder you're so thin. Sit down, I'm cooking you breakfast."

I'm speechless enough that I sit down at the counter in a bit of a daze. A few minutes later, a plate of food is pushed in front of me, and my mouth waters. I'm used to buying scraps of meat, fruit that is borderline moldy, and anything cheap enough for me to afford. These are more expensive, rare even, and the spices alone would have cost me an entire month's wage. Fluffy pancakes, bright fruits and bacon are piled on my plate, and I gulp as I cut a piece up.

"Thank you," I tell Lorenzo just before I

take a bite. By the goddess, I forgot how good food is supposed to taste.

"I've changed my mind. Lorenzo is very welcome here," Posy announces behind me. I turn to see her sitting in a fluffy pink bed with a pile of expensive meat sticks she is chewing on. What the fuck? She looks at me in disgust. "You, on the other hand, are not. Haven't you got work or anywhere else to be?"

"Good morning to you too," I mutter, turning back to my food.

Posy likes Lorenzo… I wasn't sure she ever liked anyone. Even when Louie is here, she mostly just ignores him, and she hates Nerelyth with a passion. Lorenzo has a plate piled high with food as he sits on the stool next to me and begins to eat in silence.

I'm having breakfast with a Wyern. How is this my life now?

I ignore her to dig into my breakfast, and by the time I'm done, I find Lorenzo has easily eaten twice as much as me.

"That was really nice. Thank you again."

He looks at me and smiles. "Ah, so you have manners when you have been fed."

I smile back. "I'm going to get dressed, but

I have a question," I say. "Why did the king come to get me and not you? Or a member of the court, when it's so dangerous for you to be here."

He doesn't look at me as he replies. "When it comes to my brother, rules and laws are nothing but sticks to break as he walks over them."

"Fine, but your sister is missing, and honestly, you don't seem that bothered by it. Neither does your court."

This time, he turns and his eyes meet mine. "The court are not supporters of Solandis, and most are likely happy she is gone. She believed we shouldn't hide in the mountains anymore as outcasts and monsters to those who know only the truth of the fae. That the old laws should be forgotten and war should begin. Many of us do not want a war, and she made no qualms in telling everyone she came across how cowardly she thought they were. Solandis is my half-sister and very much like her mother, who was hated by the court in the end."

Ah, so not the king's full-blooded sister either, by the sounds of it. Where are their parents? Are they still alive? I can't believe they wouldn't have been in the talk with me about their missing daughter if they were alive. I wish I knew more rumors about the Wyerns. Maybe Nerelyth will.

"Why?"

"There will be another time for that story," he replies, going back to his food and digging his fork into a red fruit. "Wherever my sister is, you're our best chance of finding her. Ethereal City has its secrets, and so do we. Find them, Calliophe."

"I'm telling my partner everything, and she won't tell a soul. Also, I want my money now. The ten percent I was promised," I say, placing my hands on my hips.

He nods at my bookcase, where a pile of gold papers line the one shelf. A hundred thousand, I bet. My mouth goes dry as I walk over, letting the shadows of the corridor cover me as I touch the money for a moment. I look over at Lorenzo, who is still watching me, and he speaks before I can. "I can't approve of you telling the siren this. My king will not be happy."

"Well, he isn't here, is he?" I counter,

lowering my hand and hating how vulnerable I felt and looked at that moment. I've never seen money like that. The security it could bring Louie. I won't have to worry about him all of the time. That money is a life for me. A life away from the dreads of Ethereal City.

Smiling, I wipe a few tears away as I go to my room, shut the door and mentally shake myself. I have to get to work. I get dressed in my leathers, clipping two daggers to both my thighs and lacing my enchanted rope around my stomach. Lastly, I put on my leather coat and tie my pink hair up in a high ponytail, leaving a few strands out before going back into the living room and slipping on my boots. I go back to the shelf and grab a bunch of gold papers, tucking some into my boots along with my keys in my back pocket before facing Lorenzo, who has cleaned up and is now sitting on the sofa, Posy sleeping curled up in her bed like a cat.

"See you later. There is a key in the bathroom, under the white stone by the sink. Lock up before you leave," I say.

"I won't be here tonight, but someone

will," he replies, spreading his long arms out. "Going to miss me?"

Truthfully—yes. I like having breakfast made for me and having someone here Posy doesn't ignore or hate other than me. "No."

He laughs, climbing up and handing me a large envelope. "In here is a painting of my sister. There's also various things that we've done to look at the hybrids that we killed. Details about them, what we suspect they were before they were changed into hybrids. Just random things I've found and information from our spies in the city on the hybrids they have encountered."

"Thanks. It will help," I reply, taking it from him and tucking it under my arm. He touches my shoulder before I walk away, and I look back at him.

He crosses his beefy arms. "You'll be watched, and if you're in trouble, just call for help. Someone will come and help."

"I can handle myself. Thanks."

I feel his eyes on me as I walk away. "I'm over a hundred and four years old, Calliophe, and even I would take caution with this."

I look back at him, nodding once before leaving him in my apartment.

I feel full, unsurprisingly, as I head down the stairs to Louie's apartment, heading inside with the key hidden in the flower pot outside. He is at school or on his way there, and I quickly check on my foster mom before leaving ten gold notes and a quick letter explaining not to go crazy with it and I'll explain later. A hundred thousand isn't enough to wake up his mom, but two hundred thousand would be.

I can do this.

For Louie.

For my foster mom and everything I owe her.

Locking up, I leave her apartment and take the twenty-minute walk back to the Enforcer Guild, hoping it doesn't rain. I rush up the steps as thunder echoes in the distance, and I'm not too surprised to find Nerelyth waiting outside for me, fully dressed in black leathers that match mine and her boots with daggered heels. I need to borrow those boots. Well, borrow and never give back until she steals them back. Her arms are tightly crossed, her red hair braided back, and she looks furious as she taps her foot on the stone as I rush up to her.

"What the hell happened to you? First with my birthday and not turning up and then you don't turn up for work? I tried your apartment, but I only found Posy and her random chatter about monster fucking," she rants, her eyes slightly glowing and her skin near shining with her power. "I was really getting worried, Calli. For a second, I even thought about singing in every part of the city until I found you."

She flings her arms around me and squeezes me tight. "I was always told not to be friends with mortals, and then you turned up, pink hair and all, and you're my best friend. You can't disappear like that."

She whacks me on the arm as she steps back. "Ouch, but I love you too, bestie. Can I talk now and explain?"

"Did you really fuck a monster?"

"Posy is insane," I mutter, noticing the guards are listening in, and one of them has very red cheeks. "We should go and talk somewhere else."

"Gotcha," she nods in agreement, hooking

her arm through mine as we walk in. We both say hello to Wendy before going through past both of our offices, which are nothing more than small desks in box rooms, and into the interrogation room. The soundproof room is bright, and it takes a second to adjust my eyes to the light as I lock the door behind us.

Nerelyth perches on the table as I start explaining everything that happened. By the end, her mouth is wide open, and she's utterly speechless.

Sagging after unloading all that, I lean against the wall. "I'm really fucked, aren't I?"

"They are Wyerns…," she whispers, clearly shocked.

"If I don't find this princess or solve this hybrid case, I think that the king might actually kill me," I say, rubbing my head. Another headache is already building. I used to get them a lot as a kid, but I haven't had any in years. I'll have to stop off at the healers on the way home tonight. Maybe stress brings them on… not that I'm usually stress free.

"They're not going to kill you. I won't let them," she says fiercely. "And it doesn't matter.

We will find this princess and who is making the hybrids."

"Thank you," I softly say, feeling like a weight has been lifted from my shoulders by just telling her this all and knowing she has my back. "I'm surprised you even believe me. It sounds like a crazy nightmare."

"Even you, my friend, are not creative enough to make this up," she says with a small laugh. "And I'm happy to know you didn't pick up a male who looks like a monster for a one-night stand. Posy had me worried about your judgment for a second there."

I laugh, shaking my head. "Posy actually likes the prince who slept on my sofa last night."

"I'm not sure many can say they had a Wyern King kidnap them and a Wyern Prince sleeping over," she says with a smile that drops for a moment. "It's going to be okay. The money... you need it for Louie and his mom. For you to finally get out of this dump."

"I'll share it with you for helping," I say quickly.

"No," she sharply replies with an echo of

power in her voice that laces a chill down my spine.

My eyes widen, and she looks away for a moment.

I clear my throat. "Okay, but the offer is there. Partners for life?"

"Always," she replies with a sad smile. "Sorry, I shouldn't have snapped like that."

"One day, if you ever want to tell me your secrets, I'll listen," I reply, pushing off the wall. "No pressure."

"Maybe one day," she repeats. "By the way, the boss has called a meeting. He was really pissed that you weren't here yesterday. I told him that you were sick, but I don't think he bought it."

"He wouldn't," I mutter. "He was mad about the hybrid and gave me a big lecture."

"It's a damn shame he talks so much with that pretty face of his."

I chuckle and look at the door. "Do you think there is any way he will believe the sick story from me?"

"Nope," she quietly replies, coming over and resting her head on my shoulder for a moment. "But screw him. You've done worse than missing a day of work, and he hasn't fired you yet."

True. Very true. I unlock the door, and we both head out together, passing the offices before making our way upstairs to the boss's floor and greeting a few enforcers we pass. There are at least fifteen enforcers already here, many looking bored as they wait around the room for the boss. We take a space beside the window, and I cross my arms as more enforcers flock into the room and fill the space.

About ten minutes later, the boss walks in, and even his footsteps seem moody. He looks around the room and pauses when he finds me. For a moment, I think he looks relieved before his lips turn into a thin line and he looks away. I don't miss the disappointment before he does. The boss isn't alone. All I see is blond hair over the whispering crowd before he stops next to my boss, and Merrick nods at him. He's fae, the newcomer. His crystal blue eyes, pointed ears, and the posh forest green uniform make it clear he is one of the queen's army, along with the royal sigil on his arm and the deadly green-bladed sword strapped on to his back. Not that he needs weapons to kill us all. His skin shimmers with power, like the glittering sea when the sun is at its highest.

"What's he doing here?" Nerelyth whispers to me.

Whatever it is, I have a bad feeling about this.

"Everyone quiet," the boss demands, and we all go silent. "This is the commander of the Queen's Royal Army. Commander Trask."

Everyone goes silent for an entirely different reason. "The commander here has a mission for us all. It's very important, so I suggest you listen."

He steps forward and puts his hands on the chair in front of him, leaning forward to look at all of us. His eyes flicker on me for a moment before continuing on until he has looked at us all. I wonder if he can see into our souls. I'm sure it's just a rumor I've heard about the great commander of the queen's armies. "As you all are aware, there are new monsters in the city. Hybrids. They're dangerous. They've killed many mortals there, causing havoc, and last night, they broke into one of the Royal Cities. They kidnapped the queen's grandson, who's ill equipped to fight."

I look at Nerelyth, who looks as shocked as me. "They came in a massive group and killed many fae. Those who were attacked were all young, and it was a party full of females and males that do not fight. They were completely outnumbered. The news will be spread throughout Ethereal City by midday, but until then, you are not to speak of this."

Deaths of any fae are seen as a great tragedy to our world. There will be mourning funerals across the entire city for months. "Why are you telling us this?"

I glance at the male enforcer who asked, one I don't know, at the same time everyone else does. He goes as red as his hair, but the commander answers, "Each one of you is going to be sent out to look for who created the hybrids. Who's leading them and why? Anyone that finds out or rescues the queen's grandson will be rewarded with more money than they can possibly imagine and invited into the dream palaces for the rest of their lives. Along with their families and loved ones and friends."

Whispers spread like wildfire around the enforcers, but my tongue feels like lead. "Now I will leave you to it. Your boss has any information you need. There will be more fae about in the city for a while, and they will assist you if needed. Be aware that the queen's grandson is clearly a very desired prize by many outside this city, and others will be searching for him for their own reasons."

He looks right at me, his midnight eyes sharpening before he turns and leaves.

Everyone is talking between themselves as I turn to Nerelyth, and she looks as pale as me. What are the odds of the Fae Queen wanting the same thing that the Wyern King does?

They both have loved ones missing, and they both need our help.

CHAPTER SIX

"I'll get us some drinks before we make a plan," Nerelyth suggests as we head to our offices, everyone still chattering about the fae commander and the queen's grandson missing. I don't know much about the Fae Queen's grandson—nobody does—except he is the sole heir to the throne after the queen's daughter died from fae fever. I'm so lost in my thoughts about the Fae Prince that I don't even notice Nerelyth is still talking. "The local witches are making sweet pea citrus smoothies. I can grab us one?"

"Sure. Thanks," I mutter, still thinking everything over and wondering why the hybrid leader would want to kidnap the Wyern

Princess and the Fae Prince in the same week. What is his or her end game? How are they making hybrids in the first place? Where are they making them without attracting attention?

Who are the hybrids... because a big bunch of people going missing from Ethereal City is going to be noticed unless they are from the poor district. I need to go there and—

"I know that look. You're lost in your thoughts. I'll be back soon, hunny."

I flash her a sheepish grin before she walks off, and I head into my office, shutting the door behind me, dust filtering across the space. My old chair practically groans as I sit at my wooden desk and open up the paper folder that Lorenzo gave me. There is a beautiful painting of a female with a small glittering gold crown on her head. The Wyern Princess. She has long black hair with tips of dark purple. Her eyes are practically white, but I'd gather they're probably silver in person, and she is slim, slightly curvy, but not muscular in any way. She does have wings and the same light grey skin as Lorenzo. She is just as pretty as I'd expect their sister to be, but there is something more rebellious in her gaze, even through this painting.

I put it to the side and start reading through the notes on the hybrids. Most of it I already know from my own research and from the three I've caught. They're always tall, grotesque and strong. Lorenzo notes they are stronger than Wyerns in combat, which means stronger than fae too. He also notes that their magic doesn't work on them. It bounces off their thick skin like the Snake Kind.

Lorenzo also notes that he thinks most of these were mortals and not supernaturals before they were changed into hybrids. By the goddess. One thing that draws my attention the most about the notes is a symbol drawn at the bottom of the page. A strange mark that looks like a triangle with a star in the middle and a tiny dot right in the center. I read what he's written on every creature, and this mark is always on their backs.

"I've shown it to Emerson. Neither of us knows much about it, but it looks like one of the old fae marks of the old language of this world."

I blow out a breath. That language is ancient, and only the old fae—like the queen

—know how to speak it. I lean back in my chair. There are rumors that some Snake Kind are said to still speak in the old marks, some of them, but getting any of them to speak to an enforcer is not going to happen unless I arrest one of them. The problem with the Snake Kind is they are slippery, and their families are a tight-knit bunch. The Snake Kind is the only race other than fae and Wyern that doesn't have bastard children living in foster care or on the streets of the poorest district. I used to wish I was one of them, years ago, when my monster was hunting me and I thought they might have been able to protect me from him.

I need to stop off at the library on my way home and find any book on the old marks and a book on Wyern history. I don't know enough about them to have one sleeping in my apartment every night. My mind flickers to some old marks sketched onto the walls of the market not far from here, but I don't think any of them were the same as this one. Still, someone who did them must be able to read this old mark.

I turn to the last page just as my door is knocked twice and opens. I barely get everything shoved inside the folder before I close it shut and lean an elbow on it, looking as casual as possible as my boss walks in. "The boss in the servants' quarters. What a high honor."

He crosses his arms. "Do you ever speak without a great deal of sarcasm?"

"Nope. Life would be boring without sarcastic people like me," I reply with a grin that he doesn't return.

"Be ready in ten. We're going out," he smoothly commands.

"So you're not here to tell me off about yesterday?"

"Will you truthfully tell me why you weren't in? I assumed, because of Miss Mist's birthday, that you drank too much," he coldly replies. "Which, Miss Sprite, is not an excuse I wish to hear at this present moment."

I sigh, and he arches an eyebrow before he leaves. I want to desperately correct him that I wasn't hungover and simply chose not to come in, just to wipe off the smug, all-knowing expression that will be plastered on his face, but I can't. It's better he thinks I'm a shit enforcer with a hangover than working for the Wyern King. Nerelyth comes back with bright green drinks a few minutes before I have to leave, and I don't have much time to ask her to look for any information on old marks before I explain the boss wants me and I have to go.

I stroll outside into the burning sunlight, where Merrick is waiting for me, tapping his shoe on the ground. He moves the second I come to his side and takes the steps two at a time, so I have to walk fast to keep up. He is silent as we head through the market, many people turning to look at him and bursting into whispers. I'm not that surprised he gets this reaction. He is only thirty years old, from what I've been told, and yet his record for monster captures is in the hundreds. High hundreds.

There's a reason why he's my boss, after all. Some say that he took down a betrayer of the queen, and they are friends. I'm not sure that is true, though.

"So, are you telling me where I'm going? Or is it just going to be a fun surprise?"

We walk around a corner and into a connecting alleyway that cuts across to the next street, and it's empty of anything but a few boxes. He adjusts his shirt as he speaks. "Roughly two weeks ago, a ship full of mortals went missing. They had been making regular trips to Goldway City, and apparently it docked as usual, but the whole ship was empty. My friend, a siren high up in the command line, claims there was nothing on his end."

"Completely empty?" I ask, furrowing my brow. "How did it even dock?"

"The ships are built with the trees from the Hollow Lands, and the wood is laced with magic. The ship can take itself home," he reminds me.

I cross my arms. "How many are missing?"

"There were at least a hundred and fifty people on board. Not counting stowaways or anyone they picked up for passage over from Goldway."

"By the goddess," I whisper. "How is that news not spreading around the city?"

"Right now, being kept quiet, along with the fae news," he answers. "We don't have long before it will become public."

"This ship certainly sounds like it's connected to our case," I say. "We need to search the ship with enchantments. I don't have any on me, but—"

"We can't get near the ship without the

captain of the port's permission," he tells me. I've been lucky not to have many dealings with the captain of the port, but as far as I've heard, he isn't a nice male.

"Alright," I say, lowering my arms. "Let's find him."

"I sent a Flame with a message an hour ago, and he agreed to meet with us," he tells me as we begin to walk. "Be alert. If he has something to do with this case, he will not allow us access, and we may be in for a fight."

"Yes, boss," I agree.

It takes us half an hour to get down to the port, even with his brisk pace. Sweat trickles down the back of my neck by the time we get there, and the port is very busy. It's bustling with fishermen bringing nets up, cleaning fish and putting them for sale, along with customers waiting to buy. I ignore the terrible smell of this place, another reason I avoid jobs down here. Even so, my stomach rumbles. I love the Lilac Firefish that I tried once, years ago, and it takes me a second to realize I do have enough money to actually buy some fish if I wanted.

We head straight towards the end of the

port, the smell of fish fading into the thick salt smell of the crystal waters. The port at the end leads to a massive wooden boat storage garage that's built on the water, waves lapping up the edges and splashing the glass windows. When we get to the door, we are stopped by two guards, and they both make it clear we aren't going in. By the flash of the unnatural yellow light to their eyes, I assume they are Snake Kind. The eyes give them away, and so do the rough gold scales scattered up their arms and shoulders, and on the one male's cheek. The Snake Kind are quite deadly but known as a lower-level supernatural compared to fae. They have fangs that drip out of their mouth when they attack, filled with venom, enough to stop anyone's heart. Their body is laced with scales, and their skin is thicker than fae. It would take a lot of sheer force to kill one of them.

They say the more yellow their eyes glow, the more powerful they are. But even then, they are a small race in the entire world.

The boss steps right up into their space. "We have a meeting with the captain of the port."

"He got called away, sir," the one on the right responds, clenching his fist closed and looking at us both in disgust. Not everyone likes enforcers. His hair is as yellow as his eyes, slicked back into a low ponytail, and he is very thin. I also notice a part of his left ear is missing. "He sends his apologies."

"I highly doubt it," Merrick snaps, looking frustrated. "I'll send another Flame tomorrow with a time, and I expect not to be held up, or the trading you do at night, without the eyes of the queen's army watching, will become very difficult. Make sure you pass that along."

The male's eyes narrow into slits. "Yes, sir."

The boss leads me away, and I look around everywhere I can, wondering if there is another way to find the ship and get on board. I spot the ship hanging in the back of the garage, roped to a single port. This one is on its own, away from the others, and it's empty. There isn't a single person on the entire deck or ship. "I bet that's the ship."

"We have to do this the right way. The captain's a rich man and could cause issues for us," he replies. "Politics of being in charge. We can't just break in."

"Fine," I say with a sigh. "Tomorrow it is. If they still screw around, I'm breaking in."

"Of course you are, and as usual, I'll write the report to explain your actions," he frustratedly replies.

I try not to grin. "As always. Anywhere nice to be today, boss?"

"Researching. As I expect you to be doing," he coolly replies. "Have a good day, Miss Sprite."

"Bye, Merrick," I say.

He looks back at me, his eyes flashing with the colors of the sea for a second, and I swear his lips flicker with a smile before he disappears into the crowd. I quickly buy a few Lilac Firefish before leaving the docks and heading to the library. The library is a looming, tall building surrounded by smooth, polished crystal rocks that make a circle around the grey stone building. It's quiet, only a few people in the entrance hall as I head inside and up to the top floor. The library isn't a big room, but it doesn't need to be. The books are all hidden. Two Flames wait at the desk in the middle of the room, and I drop two coins on the desk in front of them.

"A book on Wyern history and a book on old fae marks. Please."

The Flames look at each other, both grabbing a coin and disappearing. They reappear moments later, a book in their hands, and they drop them for me where the coins were. "Thanks."

I grab the books and leave, looking back to find the Flames' creepy eyes watching me. I will never like those things. The blistering sun beats down on me on my way back, the unseasonably warm day making me wish I didn't wear leathers. By the time I get home an hour later, I'm feeling pretty tired as I climb the stairs and go straight to Louie's apartment.

"Good timing, I just got home from school," Louie tells me as he rushes over for a hug. I hug him tightly, needing it. He steps back quickly, and I wipe some mud off his cheek. This kid always has mud on him. "What work did you do to get that kind of money?"

"Something big. That was a down payment, but if it goes well, we might be able to wake your mom up," I tell him. His eyes widen, filling with unshed tears. My heart pounds as I bite back the sob in my throat. "I'm going to do this work, and then we are waking her up. We are going to get out of here and go to Junepit City for the rest of our lives. Far away from this place."

"Really?" he whispers before throwing his arms around me once again.

I rest my head on top of his and sigh. "Really, kid."

"Just don't die. I—I don't know what would happen," he whispers back to me.

I'd do anything not to die and leave him alone. He is too young for this conversation. "I'm not going to die, and I'm not leaving you. Ever. Right, I have fish for us to cook. Something special."

"Sounds nice," he replies, his voice still haunted by his fear. I hate that he has to live like this. Louie tells me about his long day as we head to the kitchen and he cuts up some vegetables. "Macie's dad didn't come back from his journey, and she is worried," Louie says as I finish cutting the fish into chunks and head to the fire to light it.

"Oh? Where did he go?"

"To Junepit City," he tells me as I load the

fish into the steamer above the fire with the vegetables.

"I'm sure he has gotten caught up in the forests somewhere," I softly tell him.

"Can I take some of this fish to Macie's house tomorrow? They don't have much and—"

"Yes," I tell him, and his eyes brighten. "And tell her I hope her dad gets back soon."

I'm assuming her dad is one of the brave travelers who makes the trip through the ancient forests to the coast where ships await for Junepit City. The forests are older than any of us, mortal or supernatural, and the creatures within them are even older.

And deadlier.

I go check on Mom as the food cooks, and nothing is different, and yet it feels like it is, because I'm that step closer to waking her up. I eat my food with Louie as he explains the new star map the teacher has bought and how they are studying it for the next few weeks.

"For the next few weeks, can you not come to my apartment at night? And on the weekends, I'll be away. Just for a while for this job," I tell him as I finish cleaning up.

"Alright," he replies with a smile. "I'll miss you, but I have to watch the stars in the evening, anyway."

"Don't go to bed too late," I fondly say.

"Promise," he grins, and I laugh, having the sneaky suspicion he will be going to bed late.

I walk out and climb the stairs illuminated with an orange light from the setting sun, and head to my apartment.

"Hey, Lorenzo," I shout out as I step inside and remember he said it wouldn't be him here. "Or whatever bat dude is here tonight."

No one replies and I look around, finding Posy sleeping in her new bed and snoring lightly. My bed creaks and I frown, walking over and pushing the door open.

There is a monster on my bed. Again. The Wyern King.

CHAPTER
SEVEN

It's just like a flashback to the first time we met. A monster sitting on my bed, reading my book. I glare at him as he leans back on my pillows, his wings splayed over my sheets.

And he is reading my book. I recognize the red leather-bound cover and the title in black, noting it as the memoirs of Daisy Blue.

Which I'm certain is a made-up name for the fae female who wrote this book.

"This female lived an interesting life. Unlike you," he drawls before reading the book out loud. "'He was watching. My mate. In the shadow as the soldier's hot tongue swirled around my—'"

"Enough!" I demand, stepping closer and reaching for the book. He easily moves the book out of my reach and snaps it shut. "Give it back."

"No," he replies with a smirk, climbing off my bed on the other side. "I will say, neither her mate nor lovers know much about how to please her for long. Does she find any new lovers?"

"Maybe," I mutter with red cheeks. "And I think she enjoys them plenty."

He chuckles low, his amethyst eyes glowing. "Are you this bored with your life that this book is the closest you get to sex?"

I cross my arms. "Why do you care about my sex life?"

He looks me up and down with a bored expression. "I never said I did, Doe."

Sighing, I move away and click my fingers for the rest of the lights to turn on. "Why are you here, King Eveningstar? Surely you can send one of your minions to stay here tonight."

He doesn't answer me, and instead he picks up one of the seven tiny glass spheres that are on little stands on my dresser. The one he picks up is filled with sand, and it swirls on its own with a tiny starfish at the bottom. "Do you collect them?"

The king wants to know about my hobby? "Yes."

He arches an eyebrow. "Where is this one from?"

"My last foster dad gave me that one for a birthday," I answer, my heart tugging with the memory, "before he was murdered by someone with bat wings."

I don't know why I say it, but he sharply looks at me. "Did you ever find who killed your foster families?"

I tilt my head. "So you know about my past?"

"I know everything about your past and present, Doe. Along with the fact you told your partner, the siren, about our deal," he coldly replies, his voice dripping with venom. "If she breathes a word to anyone, I'll kill her myself."

"Touch her and I'll destroy you like all the monsters I've met," I breathe out.

His eyes darken and a low growl echoes from his chest. "Try me, Doe."

We both stare at each other as I shake with anger, and he seems equally pissed at me. He is the one that moves first, putting down my sphere on its stand. I half expected him to break it, and I don't know how I'd react to that. Each one of them was given to me as a gift, and they are irreplaceable because the magic that it takes to make them is unique.

"Get dressed. We have somewhere to be. Wear the purple dress," he demands, walking past me, and I step aside.

"You went through my clothes?"

"Your underwear drawer was my favorite," he calls back as he leaves my room, and I frustratedly slam the door behind him. I swear I hear him talking to Posy as I pull my wardrobe open and see the short purple dress left out. I'm not sure it fits anymore, and it's ridiculously thin material, one of the reasons I wore it once and never again. It will outline any hidden weapon on my thighs or under my dress. I ignore the temptation to wear something else only because I'm curious about where he wants to take me and wonder if it is to do with the case. It has to be to do with the case, or he wouldn't be here.

I quickly get dressed and pull my hair out, letting my pink locks fall around my shoulders in waves. I draw black lines on my eyelids, flickering out, and purple eyeshadow to match the dress. The boots I choose have a hidden dagger in the heel, and I feel better wearing them so I'm not unarmed.

Emerson is sitting on my sofa, his thighs spread wide and his thick arms resting on the back of the sofa. His horns look silver in the light, a stark contrast to his smooth, straight black hair. He watches me walk out, and his eyes very carefully trail up my legs, over the curve of my hips, all the way up to my face, where he pauses. His jaw tightens and something heated flashes in the deep amethyst glow of his eyes.

He stands up and tilts his head towards the door. "Let's go."

I glance at Posy, who is still sleeping or pretending too. "Where are we going?"

"Most mortals would die for questioning me half as much as you do," he growls.

"Do you dislike mortals as much as your court does?"

I got the funny suspicion none of them like mortals other than Lorenzo, but they are happy to have them in their beds. Typical supernatural males.

"Mortals betrayed my kind many years ago. Do not think our dislike comes from nowhere, Doe."

We betrayed them?

How?

When?

"How old are you?"

"Older than you," he counters as I step outside my apartment and he follows me out. "But I have ruled my race for five hundred years. I was king since I was eight."

"That's young to take a throne," I softly say, my own voice surprising me, along with the sadness I feel for him. I try to ignore the fact he is five hundred and eight years old. No wonder he looks at me like I'm irrelevant. I guess every mortal is when you live forever and we die so easily. "Was that when your father died?"

"He isn't dead," he coldly states. "Enough questions, Doe. You're giving me a headache."

I open my front door and look out. It is empty. Not that I see my neighbors often. Enforcers are always working odd hours. He steps out after me, hitting his wings on the sides of the doorway. I wonder if that hurts.

I look at the monster before me. The Wyern King who I know so little about but suspect so much. He looks like a warrior at this moment, all leather and glittering swords on his back. I doubt he needs the swords with the magic he has, but I bet he is deadly in any form of a fight.

He looks at me strangely, defensively, like he didn't mean to tell me anything, and I suspect he didn't. Emerson looks up, and I follow his gaze to the broken skylight. Someone's attempted to tie a blanket over it, but it's half blown away in the wind, and the sound echoes down the stairs. My breath is completely taken from my lungs when he abruptly grabs me, pulling me against his hard body, and he shoots up the stairs. I'm forced to wrap my arms around him to hold on, my fingers touching his sword and his body feeling hot against me. His hand comes to the back of my head, and he almost cradles me, like I might jump out of his arms. I'm not that crazy.

I breathe in his intoxicating scent as he whispers in my ear. "Most of my kind like to take mortals high in the sky and drop them for fun. But don't worry, I haven't done that in years."

My heart lurches through fear while his dark chuckle echoes around me as he shoots out of the skylight into the night sky. He has to be joking. Right? I keep my head plastered against his chest, my arms wrapped tightly around him and my eyes shut. I do not want to see how high we are.

The cold air whips around me as he flies fast through the sky, and I start to shiver in the dress, my lips feeling like ice. Thankfully, it's not long before my stomach's dropping and he is swooping us down to the ground where it is a little warmer. We land just outside the city, on the border edges before the open fields that lead to the ancient forests. My feet feel like jelly when he lets me go on the brown cobblestone, and I nearly fall over until I straighten myself. "For the record, I do not like flying."

"Tough shit, Doe," he replies as I run my fingers through my hair and glare at him. He looks amused as he glances at me before walking away. I shake my head and follow after him as he heads to a pair of steel doors on a stone house that sits on its own on an empty street. The door is slightly open, and he walks right up to it, pushing it further open for his wings.

This is an expensive district of Ethereal City, near the fae district, and mortals pay a fortune to live here under the fae protection. Or for the odd chance they get to see the fae—that's worth paying to live here. Apparently. I've never seen why they bother.

I follow Emerson inside what looks like a small house, but it's empty inside except for a pair of doors on the ground, smothered in a spell of some kind. The sticky sweet smell of magic fills the room, along with the icy bitterness that hangs in the air. Emerson waves his hand over the doors, and they magically open, sliding to the side and banging on the ground. My eyes widen as I get a look at the long staircase that goes deep into the ground below the doors. Emerson goes in first, and I trail after him, looking over his wings so I'm able to see where we're going.

Slowly music floats to my ears, getting louder with every step, and it gets warmer too. Eventually we come out to a massive basement with gold-painted pillars stretching for miles, and it is cram packed full of people. It's not just mortals, but supernaturals of nearly every kind fill the basement, and I don't know where to look first. Many are dancing to the rich and distinct beat of the pianissimo music as it fills my ears, and goose bumps litter my skin. I stare at a mortal male and fae female ahead of us, their bodies plastered to each other, their lips locked like it's just them and no one else. I've never let myself get close enough to anyone to feel like that. I'm not sure that even exists for someone like me. I've been to places like this, in popular bars, but it's not like this. This is so much more. Nerelyth would love it.

Spheres of light hover and move around the ceiling of the room, cascading streams everywhere in a mixture of colors, and the light reflects off the dresses of the females. The edges of the room are lined with couches and seating areas filled with people, as waiters walk around in all silver, carrying drinks. Emerson picks up two drinks off a waiter, who barely blinks at a Wyern in Ethereal City, before he continues on his way. Emerson downs both the drinks before putting his hand on the middle of my back. His palm feels like it burns straight through my dress. "Be a good doe and don't talk."

"Why bring me here, then?" I harshly whisper back, seeing red. Be a good doe? What the fuck?

He grunts and doesn't answer me, typical, as he starts to lead me through the crowd, around the dancers and past the seating area at the back. I'm sure I spot Wyern wings in the crowds for a moment, but we are moving too quickly, so I don't get long enough to look. I'm still tempted to kick him as he leads me to the back of the room and stops in front of another pair of doors. These are guarded by two more Snake people with wiry blond hair, and instead of sneering, they incline their heads to Emerson. Sometimes it's easy to forget he is a literal king.

They open the door, and Emerson all but pushes me along with him as we head inside. The small square room is empty other than a male sitting on a red leather couch. The couch matches the deep red walls and shiny red tile floors. A very expensive black suit is melded to his body, and an odd purple bow tie rests under his chin. He has braided hair that runs down his one shoulder, and it is a beautiful shade of purple, no doubt dyed, and now I see why Emerson wanted me to wear the purple dress.

I'm here as a pretty distraction. It takes a lot of effort not to stab him instead of kick him this time, and I slam my lips together, clenching my fists. I should take it as a compliment that he thinks I'm pretty enough to distract a male like this. He reeks of power, slimy and cold, and he isn't shy about letting the room trickle with his magic. Emerson might command power, but he doesn't need to show it off like this male is.

He is Snake Kind, this male. His yellow, glowing eyes are nearly luminescent, and gold scales are glittering down his cheek to his neck. Despite that, he's actually very good looking for the Snake Kind. That's rare. He stands up and bows his head at Emerson before looking over at me with a cool smile.

His voice is like a snake wrapping around your throat. "I prefer purple hair."

I clear my throat. "I prefer pink."

He laughs low and sits back down, crossing one leg over the other. "It's been a long time since you turned up here to grace us with your presence. Does she know you're here?"

Emerson's hand slips from my back, and he crosses his arms. "Still as scheming as ever. Doesn't it get boring in your old age, Grimshaw?"

Grimshaw picks at his collar, unbothered. "To what do I owe the pleasure of your company? And who is your gorgeous friend?"

"My name is Calliophe," I introduce myself before Emerson can. Grimshaw's lips spread in a big grin, and he looks between Emerson and me for a moment.

"A deep pleasure. Please sit," he muses, and two chairs appear opposite him from thin air. Snake Kind can't make magic, so that must be a well-paid-for enchantment. It hits me where I have heard the name Grimshaw before—from the wanted posters in the entrance hall of the Enforcer Guild main building. He's well known throughout all of Ethereal City as being the Snake Kind's leader, in a sense, as they have never had one before. He is known for killing, being ruthless and very dangerous. There is a list of bounties on his head higher than anyone else's I've seen. Bringing him in would be a hell of a paycheck, but no one's brave enough to do it, and the few enforcers I know that have gone after him have all ended up dead. He's a different kind of monster, one the city and the queen are willing to ignore to avoid a rebellion.

It takes a lot of will to not let my legs shake as I take the seat Emerson holds out before he sits next to me, directly opposite Grimshaw. His wing brushes against my arm, and strangely, I find it a little comforting.

"We need to talk," Emerson begins, leaning back in his seat.

Grimshaw's seedy eyes are on my legs as he replies. "What about?"

Emerson follows his line of sight, and his body goes rigid with tension. "There's very few in the world that know the old language of the fae marks, because most of it was transcribed by the Snake Kind for the royals. I know it was mostly written by your ancestors specifically, and that language was never lost to your family."

"Interesting history lesson, King Emerson," he taunts.

"You can read the marks, so what is this?"

Emerson pushes over a piece of card. The fae mark that was on the hybrids is drawn in the center.

Grimshaw glances at it once. Just once and very quickly. He has seen it before. "That's a piece of information that's going to cost you heavily."

Emerson's voice is like ice. "What do you want?"

Grimshaw's eyes roll up and down me. "I want her."

I go very still, my heart racking up a beat in my chest. I don't expect Emerson's next words. "She is mine. Don't look at her. Don't speak to her. Don't even think about it."

I sharply look at Emerson, but his gaze is locked on Grimshaw's like a predator locking onto his prey. Grimshaw laughs deep and low. "Then get the fuck out of my place."

Emerson doesn't move, and the tension in the room is thick. I clear my throat and place my hand on Emerson's arm.

He snaps his head to me. His eyes are no longer purple but glowing a radiant white. Like two stars. "There must be something else you want. Trust me, I'd just be a hassle for you, and there are plenty of willing females in the city."

Grimshaw's eyes take everything in. "You would be a prize, Calliophe."

The growl that echoes in the room is frightening, but the steely, haughty tone of Emerson's voice is worse. "She is, and she is mine."

I dig my nails into Emerson's arm, looking deeply into his eyes that haven't once faded from the glowing white stillness. "We should leave. We will find another way."

"How much fae runs in your blood, Calliophe?"

I turn back to Grimshaw. "I haven't got a clue. Not a lot, I'd bet."

He hums low. "Pink eyes are a rare trait among the fae. How many have you seen before? They are always purple- or blue-eyed and fair-haired."

I hadn't noticed as I don't spend much time with the fae. It might be weird, but it's the least of my worries at the moment.

"Stop being a dick," Emerson growls, but he sounds like he has snapped out of the possessive alpha asshole attitude he just got into. "And a coward. What is the mark?"

Grimshaw's eyes tighten. He didn't like being called a coward one little bit. "This is dangerous shit to be involved in, Emerson."

Emerson stands. "Do I look like I give a fuck?"

"You might not, but unless I want to end up where your sister is, I'm not saying fucking anything about this."

In a blink, Emerson is across the space, his large hand wrapped around Grimshaw's neck, holding him against the wall as he struggles. In the next second, Emerson's fist pounds into Grimshaw's face. Once, twice... three times before he steps back, but Grimshaw stays hovering on the wall, held by invisible magic. The icy sting coats my tongue as Emerson wipes Grimshaw's blood off his knuckles and looks over at him. "Any friendship we had is fucking done. If I find out you had anything to do with this, your death will be slow and painful."

Grimshaw lands in a thud on the couch, gasping for air as Emerson takes my hand and pulls me to the door. He kicks it open, the doors slamming out, and the guards are piled on the floor. He knocked them out with magic, without even needing to be in the room.

"The tides are turning, King Emerson. You can't hide in those mountains forever! Time is ticking!"

Keeping a hold of me, Emerson doesn't look back; he doesn't even stop as he lunges through people, pushing some out of the way, while others simply run to move out of his path.

I soon realize we're not heading towards the exit, as he pulls me right into the middle of the dancers and tugs me tightly against him. I freeze in his arms, all of his hard body pressing into me, and I feel so small in his arms. He sinks his hand into my hair and shocks me further by moving us to the music. I look into his eyes, my heart racing. "What in the goddess are you doing?"

He leans down, his tough but somehow soft lips brushing the tip of my ear. "I believe my sister knew something about all of this. Every answer is in this room."

"We are dancing so you can listen in?"

"I can listen to every conversation," he whispers back to me, my hips swaying against him. He controls my body to the music, and I can't breathe with how close he is to me. His voice changes, dipping deeper and seductive, a voice the goddess herself would struggle not to be seduced by. "Everyone knows you're mine by the end of this dance. It will make you untouchable in this city. In the world."

I feel dizzy and breathless. "You're claiming me so that I'm protected while I look for your sister."

"Of course," he hums, his voice sending shivers rippling everywhere. "Why else would I claim a mortal as my own?"

Like a cold bucket of water is poured over me, I swiftly turn my gaze to him. He is my enemy, most likely knows who hunted me as a child and killed everyone I loved. I can't trust him, and he clearly hates mortals as much as I hate monsters.

So when he suddenly kisses me, I hate myself for how my body responds.

I burn to life.

His lips part my own with a tender pressure as he claims control, dominating the kiss with every brush, every stroke until there is nothing but him.

He pulls away and steps back, his eyes dark purple stars in the darkness. I've never been kissed like that before. Not once.

And he is a monster.

Emerson takes my hand without another word and leads me outside. I know the kiss was all for show, but still, I step into him before he can tug me close, and he shoots us both into the night sky.

CHAPTER EIGHT

My stomach is still turning like a million butterflies are swirling around within it as I walk on shaky legs to my front door and head inside my home. My monster following, of course. Emerson follows me in, shutting it behind him with a slam loud enough to wake up the entire building. I resist the urge to mention he is paying to fix the door if he breaks it. I stop by the kitchen as he walks past me, each step confident and easy like he has lived here his entire life. Maybe it's because he is a king... maybe it's because he is just Emerson. He owns every room he walks into. His wings are like shadows behind him as he heads into my bedroom, and he doesn't slam that door shut.

I look at the empty room in pure shock and confusion for a moment before shaking my head. I'm too tired for his bullshit tonight. I slip off my boots just as Posy whips through the air around my head, skating by my ears, and landing on the counter. She hangs herself upside down on the cabinet, and her doe eyes have an evil twinge to them tonight. I'm way, way too tired to deal with her at the moment.

"Did you run out of bats to fuck?" she muses with a haughty laugh. "If so, can you bring the other one back? The prince. I like him."

"So you know he's prince of the Wyerns?" I question. Is she aware that the bat she is making fun of is the king?

"I'm well aware who the Wyerns are," she coolly replies. Her voice is full of contempt for everything and everyone, but especially me. "Your ward came today to check on you, and he might be worried."

I blink in surprise. "Thanks."

She closes her eyes. "Keep it down with bat dude. Some of us need our beauty sleep."

I suck in a breath. "Sometimes I think you're my friend and that the years of looking after you might have finally made you look at me and realize I'm your friend. That I'm the only one in this world in your corner. I know that you're pissed because a witch did this to you, and I can't change that. I know you're angry at everything, at life, but hating me and arguing with me and pushing me away will end up with only you being alone. Do you understand that?"

I regret most of the words the moment I say them. I know it's because I'm tired and confused and my life is turning into madness. A madness that involves kissing monsters as I chase other monsters.

A part of me, a small part that is selfish, thinks about just leaving her and not taking her with me. She clearly hates me. But then I remember the truth of why I never will do that. She was once broken, injured, alone on the streets and begged for my help. She begged and pleaded, even as I helped her. Just for the pain to stop, for the witch to end the curse, for her life back. She's snarky, cruel, but it's all a facade to hide how she really is. Because I've seen her kindly whispering to Louie when he has had a bad day at school. Because when I was sick with the fae fever, she was the one that talked me through it. I don't know if I would have survived without her. She was kind to me, and even when I'm angry at her, like right now, she is my family.

Posy might hate the world for what she's become, but I hope, one day, she will realize that we would never have met without her being cursed.

Her voice is soft and filled with unspoken pain. "I was once... Once I would never have even spoken to someone like you."

I turn back to her, frowning. "What is that meant to mean?"

She doesn't answer, flying off her perch and into the shadows near the sofa, clearly done with this conversation. I'm sure that was some kind of insult, anyway. I rub my forehead as I walk to my room, feeling so tired my eyes are drooping.

I pause in the doorway, seeing the monster king lying on my bed, shirtless. Any thoughts of anything else other than the muscular chest in front of me and the monster lying on my bed drift away until there is this sense of déjà vu. His boots are kicked off on my floor at the end of the bed, his thick arms are behind his head, and he looks like he has lived here forever. Only he is too big for my bed, dwarfing the double, and there is no way he is sleeping there. I lean against the doorframe and cross my arms. "Get out of my bed, Emerson."

"I feel like we keep doing this on repeat. You tell me to get out of your bed or room. I don't listen," he muses, his voice gravelly and deep.

I narrow my eyes. "Well, it wouldn't be on repeat if you actually did listen and get out. I'm sleeping here, and you can sleep on the sofa."

"That is unlikely," he dryly responds. "My brother is a gentleman, but I am not. I'm sleeping here."

"Fine. I will sleep on the sofa," I all but shout in annoyance.

The fucker just laughs. "No, you won't."

With his magic, I'm pushed forward by the door, and it slams shut behind me. I spin around and pull the handle to find it's locked tight with magic. After a minute, I frustratedly growl and turn back to him. I roll my eyes and go into my bathroom, which has a door to the corridor, but it's locked, too. I storm back to the other door.

Emerson is smirking, watching me as I snap. "Open it."

His deep laugh wraps around me. "No."

By the goddess, I hate this monster.

No matter how much I pull the handle, it won't open. It is never going to open, and I've never seen magic like his. I wouldn't have a clue which enchantments to buy to counteract it. I'm not sure anything could.

I blow out an angry breath. "I'm tired, and I don't want to spend the night arguing with you."

"Then give in," he all but purrs.

My cheeks burn at his undertone, but he continues on. "We're two adults. Do you think you won't be able to sleep in this bed without keeping your hands off me?"

I'm too flustered to even control the words that fly out of my mouth. "You're the one that kissed me! It wasn't me that had trouble keeping my hands to myself!"

I expect him to deny it, but instead his voice is smug. "And you enjoyed it, Doe."

I feel that invisible tug between us for a moment, like it's wrapping around the air in the room and demanding I pay attention to it. To him.

Maybe it's his magic. Maybe he doesn't feel it at all, and it's all me. I don't know what it is, but I resist it with absolutely everything I have, even as tired as I am. He tilts his head to the side, going into stillness in a way that is unnatural and so very immortal. It's a fae thing to be so still, and every mortal instinct in me wants to run from the danger his kind exudes so effortlessly. My soul screams for me to run. My heart pounds as he watches me, and my hands feel shaky. "Are Wyerns like fae?"

He looks away. "Our ancestors are nearly the same."

"Oh," I whisper, unsure why I even asked that. "I'll just sleep on the floor, and you can have the bed. You are the guest and a king, after all."

He doesn't move or reply as I pull out a spare blanket from the drawers and grab a pillow off the bed from under his wing. I throw them both on the floor before going to my bathroom, slamming the door behind me before changing into the nicest pair of pajamas that I have. These are all black, silky, and fit to my body like a glove. I don't know why I spend a moment looking at myself in the mirror as I brush my hair.

The room is colder than usual as I head back inside and sit down. I barely lie down for a second before icy cold magic wraps around my arms and legs. Suddenly I'm floating in the air as a scream rips out of my throat, the blanket and the pillow coming with me into the air. The magic suddenly disappears, and I slam down onto the bed on my back, the blanket landing on top of me. I roll to my side and look at him in pure, undiluted shock. "What did you just do?"

His eyes are closed, his arms crossed as he lies back. "Goodnight, Doe."

"I am not sleeping in a bed with you," I frustratedly snap. I climb up off the bed, pulling my blanket and pillow with me. I hear a light chuckle right before his magic comes back again, and this time I scream in annoyance as he drops me back on the bed at his side. This time, he keeps his magic wrapped around me like a cocoon, not letting me move at all as the blanket falls over me. "There you go, little Doe. All tucked in. Good night."

I'm shaking with anger as I growl. "Let me go, you son of—"

Magic wraps around my mouth like a hand, sealing my lips shut. Oh no, he didn't. I wiggle and scream in frustration right before I hear his light snores next to me. Bastard. Eventually I give up, knowing he won't release his hold on me and I can't fight his magic forever to get nowhere when I'm so tired. I spend ages staring up at the ceiling, ignoring the blistering heat that comes from his body at my side and how comforting it feels. The icy sting of his magic seems to fade into something warmer and more lulling over time. Despite it all, I can't help but fall asleep.

A memory of sorts flickers across my eyes, a different, darker, nastier magic wrapping around me. Frozen pictures, dreaded colors, awful scents flickering across my eyes like it's happening all over again. The burning, the scraping of claws and a strange flapping of wings. All the sounds slamming into my mind over and over again until all I can see is that I'm standing in front of a house on fire, the flames stretching high into the sky. Like they could touch the stars themselves. I'm silent and quiet as I watch the flames spread into the buildings nearby, the gardens and quiet street destroyed. My dress is burning at my feet, embers flicking around in the air, but I don't move. I never did. People scream, over and over, as I see him fly out of the flames. A male outlined in the dark with large black wings, a big, powerful form, but this time I don't run.

I ran every single time from him, and I probably should run this time. But I don't. I want to know who he is. This is the moment I stop running from him and begin hunting my monster. If he wants me dead, I'm going to face him first and learn the truth.

I only get to take one step before cold magic slams into me from behind, and everything goes black.

I wake up with my heart racing, my skin sticky with sweat, and everything is still dark around me, just like that night. I can't breathe for a moment, sucking in great gasps of air when my body realizes it can breathe.

It's not just dark. I'm wrapped in wings. Emerson's dark wings are locked around me, and I'm curled up in them, my knees pressing into his stomach and hands pressed against his chest. I slowly lift my head, finding Emerson watching me with an unreadable expression. "What did my mortal dream of?"

Strange symbols are carved into his skin under my hand, over his ribs, like they were burnt there. I gulp. "I was dreaming about when I was ten and I did something very stupid."

Maybe it's because I've just woken up, maybe it's because he is so easy to talk to like this, but I'm never vulnerable with anyone. I don't usually let people in, and I don't talk to anyone about my nightmares. Not even Nerelyth knows all of my history. She knows some of it but not all the little parts, the deep frustrating parts, the bits that scare me, scare me more than I would like to admit. The nightmares that, for some reason, I feel this monster could know. Maybe because he comes from the dark. It's there that my nightmares and my past belong.

"Tell me about it."

I blow out a breath. "There isn't much to tell."

"I doubt that," he replies, his hot breath blowing against my forehead. "For some reason, I find your mortal life interesting."

I don't know what to say to that or why it makes something in my chest warm. "What's it like to be king?"

"What's it like to work for M.A.D.?"

I know he is changing the subject, but I can't help but answer him this time. "The Monster Acquisition Division is usually a good job, and it kept me alive. Louie too. It was the only job I could do after coming out of foster care. Any other job wouldn't even look at me with no experience, no family, no money. I was quite literally coming off the streets, and they gave me a chance, plus I've always been good at running. I've run my entire life."

He stays quiet for a long time, and I'm almost sure he's not going to say anything else and go back to sleep. But instead, he lifts his hand and carefully brushes a strand of my pink hair behind my ear. "Then we have something in common. I've run from something my entire life, too."

I swear I don't breathe, and I feel like the

seconds roll into nothing until we're just looking at each other. "When do we stop?"

"You tell me, Doe."

His eyes drop to my lips for a moment before looking back up. Something in his eyes hardens when he looks right into mine, like he's reminding himself of something. Probably the fact that I'm very, very mortal and I'm working for him. He needs me to get his sister back. "You asked me what it's like to be king. It means every decision, every choice, every burden is on your back. You have to do things that you never wished or wanted to, and you don't get to be what you wish. You never get to be free like the people you protect. Everything is for the crown and for your race."

I furrow my brow. "But surely, if you're king, you can do whatever you want."

His eyes look like glittering stars in a deep purple sky. "Being king means I'm probably one of the only people in the world who can never do exactly what they want or take what they want without a price. Responsibility comes with any crown, but more with my own."

"I hope you get what you want one day,

Emerson. You might be a frustrating asshole for the most part, but no one deserves a life with nothing they want."

He laughs low and deep, and I feel his chest rattle under my hands. "Get some sleep, Doe. You have my sister to find, and I have a city to search in the morning."

"So you're looking for her, too?"

"I never said I wasn't," he replies quietly. "Better to have a team search a city than just me."

I nod. "And you have to be careful not to be seen."

"When you live in the shadows, being invisible is simply what you become."

In the darkness, in his wings, I find sleep as easy as breathing within seconds.

CHAPTER NINE

I wake up slowly, feeling less tired than I have in a long time. I actually slept well... and I'm not for a second admitting that was because of him. I shiver, surprisingly cold, and when I open my eyes, I no longer see dark grey velvety wings but instead yellow and orange light spreading across my ceiling. I would believe it was all a dream if it wasn't for his scent, which lingers in the air. Frosty dawn break, rain smothered grass and peppermint. By the goddess, he smells good.

I roll over onto the pillow he was lying on, and blink as I breathe in his lingering scent. Do I have a crush on a monster?

On the Wyern King?

I shake my head, wondering what in the goddess is going on with me as I climb up off my bed and go to the bathroom, throwing water into my eyes and waking me up. It's too early for a drink, but I think I need one if I'm crushing on the Wyern King. He is an immortal, deadly, dangerous and goes through females quickly, I bet. But I still feel his lips on mine, his wings wrapped around me, and the goddess... I need to stay away from him. I have a job to do and a princess to find. A Fae Prince too.

Then I can disappear from this city with my family.

Emerson could never be part of that plan.

I head out into the main room to see that Emerson may have gone, but he's cooked a massive breakfast. Croissants, fruit, sausages, bacon and porridge are lined up on plates. It's... sweet. There's even fresh coffee in a metal jug to keep it warm. I glance at Posy, who is in her pink bed. "Any chance the prince did this and not Emerson?" I ask.

"Did you know it's a custom for Wyern

males and fae males to serve females food before they eat?"

"No," I reply, looking at the food. "If I eat this, I don't have to marry them or something?"

I swear she laughs, but evil mortals cursed into bat forms can't do that. At least not at something I said. "If they share their food on their plate, they believe you're their mate. You're good, as he didn't eat any of this before he left."

I grin in relief, because I'm hungry, and make a mental note not to share anything on my plate with any of the Wyerns staying here. Not that they would ever want me as a mate. Mates are rare, two souls bound across time and space and every world out there to only love each other. For mortals, *mate* is simply a title, but for supernaturals... it's so much more.

I eat breakfast, trying a bit of everything before wrapping the rest up to eat later. I have a quick look at the time after getting dressed for the day and realize that I need to be getting to work soon, or I'm going to be late. I'm just tying my hair up when a Flame bursts into the middle of my lounge, right on my sofa, leaving ash stain and burn marks shaped like Flame feet.

I sigh. "Hello."

"Mortal named Calliophe Sprite, I carry a message from Merrick Night. He sends the message: Meet me now at the docks. Same place as before."

I pick up a coin off the corner of the side. "Thank you for the message."

I flip the coin up in the air, and he catches it in his teeth before disappearing into flames, ash going everywhere. I quickly clean up the best I can, but the foot marks on the sofa aren't going anywhere, and I'm sure the Flame did that on purpose. Before I tighten my thigh strap, I grab a few enchantments and my daggers. Finally, I slide my boots on before leaving my apartment and quickly making my way across the city.

I find Merrick waiting on the edge of the dock, near the captain's office, his hands tucked into his grey suit pockets that match his eyes. He is so still as he watches the horizon, his shoulders tense, and for a moment I wonder if it is even possible that he is more than a mortal. The bright sun casts a shadow down on him as he turns, and his grey eyes meet me with a reflection of the yellow sunlight, highlighting the dark flickers within them. "Hello, boss."

"You're late, Miss Sprite."

I grin and ignore his pissed off tone. "Hey, I wouldn't have been late if you hadn't demanded I come here instantly. You could have sent the Flame earlier."

He glowers at me. Someone is in a bad mood. "If you'd been at work on time, the walk wouldn't have been so far."

"Agree to disagree?"

His lips twitch, but he looks away from me and to the port where the captain's office is. He inclines his head, and we say nothing else until we get to the Snake Kind guards outside. They are the same ones that were here last time, and they both sneer at us. I ignore it, as we aren't usually liked by many in the city. We aren't heroes to them. The fae are. We just do the grunt work and sometimes annoy them when we get in their way.

This time, Merrick doesn't have to introduce himself before they both open the doors and we head inside. I steel my back and open my senses for any kind of danger, and I feel Merrick do the same, his eyes assessing every door and window for an exit.

The captain of the port is leaning by the window, watching the still green sea. A gold spyglass is held in his right hand, and his left hand rests on a sharp sword on his hip. He turns his head slightly and looks over at us. His dark green hair is braided all the way down his back, and his one eye is littered with scars. The pupil is so white that I doubt he can see out of it. The other eye is crystal blue-green, which matches the color of the sea, and I doubt for a second the rumors of this male being ruthless and as cold as the sea are exaggerating anything at all.

The rumor that he isn't all mortal is true. He is a good part fae and maybe a little siren too, if I'd take a guess. He waves a scarred hand at the two wooden chairs by a desk before he comes and sits in the large leather chair on the other side. As I sit down next to Merrick, I notice the desk is cluttered with many, many things. Swirling orbs, fish in jars, different pens, mixtures of papers in piles, and dozens of books, and it matches the chaotic room. The entire room is disheveled with things. The captain leans back in his seat, his arms crossed tight and his expression less than friendly. "What do you want?"

Merrick matches his expression with one that should downright scare any mortal. "I don't appreciate the stunt you pulled yesterday, captain."

"I was busy." The captain waves a hand in the air. "When the sea calls, I answer. Mortals must wait."

Merrick sighs low. "You know exactly why we're here. Let's not fuck about the details. I want to see the ship, and I want you to tell me what you know about it."

"We have enchantments to check it over," I add in.

The captain's eye slides to me before drifting away. "No one goes on that ship. It's haunted by the taken souls."

Merrick looks ready to ring the captain's neck. "We don't believe in haunts from old gods."

The captain laughs. "You should believe in the old gods that drift around this world. The old gods decided to take the lives of everyone on that ship, and no one else should walk upon it unless you wish to join them. I will not take anyone on board."

"I'll take our chances," Merrick dryly replies.

"No, you won't. That is my ship, and even you, Merrick Night, will not make me."

Merrick smirks, crossing his arms and touching the tips of the swords he has hidden under his suit. "Is that a bet?"

I clear my throat. I don't want this to end in a big fight, and there must be an easier way to convince him to let us on that ship. "Can you tell me which old god you believe took an entire shipload of mortals?"

Merrick's eyes whip to me, and he doesn't have to say it. He thinks I've gone crazy. No one really talks about the old gods. We talk about the dragon goddess herself because there is proof she existed, and she is buried under the fae castle. She was real, flesh and blood, magic and fae all wrapped into one. The old gods are nothing but a myth, a dark rumor of beings so powerful they could travel between the worlds and grant blessings to any they saw fit. "As far as I know, there are four old gods, each an element. There is the god of water, the god of earth, the goddess of air and the goddess of fire. Am I right?"

The captain links his fingers together and smiles at me. "At least one of you has some sense. Yes, you're correct. Some say there was even a fifth. A god of magic."

That, I've never heard of.

"When I was a young boy, I fell into the sea. I was five and I couldn't swim. I remember the water swallowing me up like I wasn't anything but a stone to it. The deep dark pits of the water took me under, and I wanted to live. As I sucked in more water, filling my lungs to the point they felt like they would explode, I begged for help. No one mortal came to save me. I was a silly boy with no family, and I walked too close to the edge of the sea when I was told not to. I remember a voice whispering into my mind, promising to save my poor mortal life if I spent the rest of it in worship of him."

"How did you escape the water?"

"I woke up on the beach the next morning, and I knew he had saved my life. I worship both the god of water and admire the goddess of air, as she has saved my perfect arse several times out at sea. They bless us on our journeys across the waters."

"The sirens ease the way and bless it," Merrick responds, his jaw tight.

The captain laughs low. "Oh, Mr. Night, that's the issue with you lot. You only believe what you can see and not what is right in front of you in the shadows, in the light, in the air and sea. Open your eyes, and you will see this world for what it really is."

Merrick glances at me with his eye twitching, and I know he is two seconds away from just dealing with this in his own way, i.e., both of us in a fight with the captain and his guards. And anyone else who comes to defend him. "Why do you think the god of water took all the mortal lives on that ship?"

The captain hums. "Sometimes the old gods decide to take the lives of those that travel around the world, those they wish to take. That is their choice as we live in their world."

"Then can it be our choice to go on board?" I softly ask. "If it is our time for the old gods to take us, then so be it."

He blows out a breath. "I will sacrifice that ship to the god of fire himself and pray that is the end of the life that is taken. That ship is unholy."

I smile at him. "We only wish for a few minutes."

"It is your choice to anger the gods if you wish it," he replies. "I can't let you walk around my port alone, but I will escort you so far."

"Thank you," I say with a beaming smile.

The captain tilts his head to the side, his eye running down me and back up. Slowly. "You are more than welcome to stay here with me tonight, darling girl, if you survive."

Merrick growls as he stands. "Do not even think about it, captain. My staff are off limits while working."

The captain looks between us and grins. "I see. The offer will always stand for you, beautiful. You remind me of the goddess of fire."

What did he mean, he sees? He sees what when he looks between Merrick and me? I frown at Merrick and the captain, who are staring each other down.

Merrick is already changing the subject.

"What can you tell us about the day the mortals went missing?"

The captain crosses his beefy arms, covered with inkings that no doubt mark him as someone who worships these gods he talks of. "The same as I told everyone that asked. The ship is enchanted to return to this port, like all my ships, but this one turned up empty. It was five days later than expected, and as far as I know, there were no storms out of the normal on the seas. It's also the wrong time of year to find creatures taking the ships, and either way, if it was a creature, they would have destroyed the ship too."

"There is no damage to the ship? No blood?" I question.

"Nothing," the captain answers. "I sent one male on board to check it out, and he disappeared not long after that."

"What was his name?" I ask.

"Condan Sayers," the captain answers. "Good lad, but young and foolish, as most males are. I wouldn't let anyone else on the ship when he disappeared the next day. The gods took him too."

I doubt it. Whoever took the mortals on the

ship, no doubt to turn them into hybrids, likely took Condan too.

"Are you sure he didn't just leave?" Merrick questions.

"He has a baby and family at home to look after. His family said he disappeared, and that was unlike him. They all live in the poor district, and without his work... well, things aren't good," the captain explains.

They will lose everything, he means. My jaw tightens and I try not to think about them. They aren't the only ones. The poor district is full of stories like that. I should know. I came from there. "Can you give me their address?"

"Ask a Flame," the captain suggests, standing up and stretching. "Come on then, I don't have much time to be wasting. The sea is waiting for me."

I follow behind Merrick and the captain as we all walk away from the desk. We head out of a side door and onto a thin wooden path made of planks, floating inches above the still water. The path leads straight towards the boat, and I look up at the imposing ship, noting how eerie it is as it floats in the water, rocking slightly. Green algae have grown up its sides, which have siren symbols drawn into the wood to protect it over the seas, and at the front is a slim female statue made of silver, stretching her fingertips out to reach nothing. It takes a few minutes for the captain to get the entrance plank to drop down in front of us, and he tests it by touching his foot before quickly stepping back.

"May the old gods bless your souls."

Merrick and I look at each other before Merrick walks up the plank, not giving a shit about the captain's warnings of old gods. In our job, we have heard so many people talk of the old gods. Most of them pray to them before they die.

I follow him up onto the ship, looking back once to see the captain standing near the plank and watching. "Foolish mortals make easy deaths for the gods."

I don't answer that warning as I head on the ship and jump onto the deck. The deck itself is simple and busy, but it looks like everyone just stopped what they were doing. Ropes and barrels are left randomly, and a compass lies on the floor by my feet, just dropped there. I lean down and pick it up, looking at the gold compass as the middle dial spins constantly.

"Look at this, boss," I say, heading over to Merrick, who is standing near the wheel of the ship, looking around. He looks down at me, and just as I take a step on the stairs to head up, I hear an echoing male scream.

"Do the enchantments! Quick!" Merrick demands as he jumps over the railing and runs past me to where the screaming is coming from. I pull the two vials out of my pocket and mix them together, making a glowing blue power swirl inside the vial. The second I pour this down, it will show me anything in the past in this place that made a burst of energy. It can be a death, a fight, or even a declaration of love.

I'm about to drop the vial when a hybrid monster jumps on the deck. The captain is held in his claw, and he shakes the captain's very dead body before looking at me. This hybrid monster is disgusting, rotting brown skin, stretched limbs, and black long claws... but I think it might have been mortal once. Its eyes are crystal blue and so very mortal.

For a moment, I wonder if there is any

mortality left in it. Until it literally rips the captain apart into pieces, blood spraying all over him and the deck, and my stomach turns. I resist the urge to throw up as I take a step back and wonder where the fuck Merrick is, while I slip out a dagger from my side. Three more hybrids jump onto the deck, and they aren't alone. A figure, hidden in a black cloak, lands next to them. He leans down in the middle of the hybrids, and his hands begin to glow. I would guess he is male, from his build under the cloak, but I'm too far away to pick up anything else.

The hybrids are protecting him.

Goddess, protect me.

"You need to make new friends. These have a bad smell!" I yell.

The hooded figure looks over, and I see a flash of golden skin right before he looks back down at the glowing orange sphere in his hands. What is that?

The only issue with attracting his attention? The hybrids all turn to me.

Three of them leap off the floor right at me, and I lunge to the side, barely missing getting my head pulled off as they rip the railing to pieces.

Another one jumps at me, knocking me straight onto my back, and I roll over to lash out with my dagger, cutting a line across his face. Black, hot, stinking blood splashes across my arm, burning me, and I hiss in pain. The hybrid screeches as I roll out of the way, and I slam my dagger into its arm, knocking it down.

But it doesn't attack me.

It runs.

I climb to my feet to see the hybrids diving into the sea and the hooded figure walking away, leaving that glowing orange orb pulsating on the deck. "Wait!"

The hooded figure looks over his shoulder, right before he jumps straight into the sea. I'm climbing down the stairs just as the orange sphere explodes. I barely get a second to scream as the world becomes flames, fire, air... and pain.

Splinters of wood cut through my clothes, and something hard slams into my head. Everything is a mixture of red, black and darkness right before I plunge into icy cold water that makes me gasp.

Suddenly I'm weightless for a second in the water, my arms floating at my sides as I look around me. Water fills my lungs, drowning me, and something is wrapped around my leg, pulling me deeper. I struggle to swim upwards, battling against the weight of whatever is wrapped around my leg, and I start to panic as a big piece of the ship falls down near me. I can see the light of the surface above me, and it's getting farther away by the second. I look down, seeing a rope wrapped around my leg, and I know I need to get it off. I reach for my other dagger, just barely slipping it out into my hand before reaching down and trying to cut through the rope with all the strength I have left. My lungs burn, and my mind races to fight the black spots in my vision as I keep cutting. The rope is too thick, and my arms are too weak.

By the goddess, I'm going to die here.

No. Please no.

I don't know if I'm already dead as I look up and see a shadow swimming for me. A shadow with wings. I barely register it's Emerson as he lunges for me and kisses me, blowing air into my mouth. The kiss lasts for barely a second as he lets me go, taking the dagger from my hand and swimming for my leg. He easily cuts through the rope, and the second it falls away from my leg, he wraps his arm around my waist and uses his powerful wings to help swim us both up to the surface. I gasp for air the second we break the surface, coughing out water and shaking as he flies us high up into the sky. I cling to him as he lands, and his hands cup my face, searching my eyes. "Breathe. You're alive. Breathe for me, Doe."

His eyes feel like they pull me back to the world, like following a constellation of stars, like a map back, as I slow my breathing down, until I can finally register that his magic is like an icy breeze spreading over my skin, kissing every little cut and bruise until nothing hurts anymore.

"You're healing me."

He doesn't say a word as he lets me go, and I finally notice we are hidden behind another ship, and there is no one around. He took a big risk saving me. "I owe you my life."

His jaw is tight. "Find my sister."

He shoots into the sky, and I feel dizzy watching until he is gone and there is nothing but thick clouds hiding the sun. I'm shivering from head to toe as I make my way off the deck and towards the crowds looking at the destroyed ship, which is nothing but flames and ash and wood floating on the sea now.

"Calliophe!" Merrick shouts, his voice full of panic.

I turn and find him on the edge of the water, searching for me. His eyes find me, and there is instant relief there as he runs to me.

"I'm good," I tell him before he starts.

He looks me over. "How are you not injured?"

I lie quickly. "I jumped into the water before the explosion, and I'm a good swimmer."

"Another skill to mark down on your impressive list," he replies with a rare smile. "What happened on board?"

"A clusterfuck," I mutter. "But someone didn't want us on that ship, and they were willing to risk being caught to destroy it." Glancing at the black blood on his suit, I ask, "Where were you?"

"Fighting two of them off. I was running to the ship when it exploded."

Nodding, I start explaining everything that happened as Merrick takes his jacket off and wraps it around my shoulders. But my mind focuses on only one thing.

King Emerson must have been watching me to be able to save me today.

CHAPTER
TEN

The walk back to the headquarters is silent, and Merrick looks lost in his own mind—and truthfully I am too. Thankfully, I'm nearly dry by the time we get to the steps, thanks to the sun coming out from behind the clouds. Merrick nods to the enforcer guards who all but bow their heads. I smile at the newbies.

Wendy gasps as I walk my wet boots across the tiles to her. "What happened to you two?"

My smile is grim as Merrick ignores Wendy altogether and walks up the stairs. Wendy, who is used to being ignored by Merrick, keeps her eyes on me. "I had to swim out of trouble today. I'm going to get changed before I turn this place into a pool."

She furrows her brow. "Are you alright? Can I get you anything?"

"You're sweet, but I'm fine, thank you," I softly tell her and head back into my office.

I've barely finished getting changed into my spare set of clothes I keep here before Nerelyth bursts in, slamming the door shut behind. "I heard that the captain of the port is dead, and a ship blew up with enforcers on it."

"Yup, I was on it," I reply, sitting down on my seat.

Nerelyth's eyes widen as she looks me over. "But you don't look hurt at all. How is that possible?"

"According to everyone else, I jumped into the sea and I'm a splendid swimmer."

"You're shit at swimming. You could drown in a puddle," she deadpans.

"True," I chuckle, wincing a little. A drowning joke is a little raw right now. "I didn't jump. The ship blew up, and I was thrown into the air and into the sea."

"Dragon goddess above," she gasps, placing her hand over her heart.

I clear my throat. "Emerson—the Wyern King—dived in and saved my life. He also used his magic to heal me."

Her eyes go even wider, and we both drop into silence. To break the silence up, I give her a quick rundown of the entire event, and by the end, she seems hyper focused on one thing. "The kiss—the life saving. How can you work for him and not fall for him after this?"

My heart jumps and I squash it down. "I don't fall in love. I don't risk it. Love is foolish and selfish, Nerry. Besides, he would never look at me as anything but the mortal he hired."

Her eyes soften. "He jumped into the sea to save you. Oh my heart."

"I wasn't expecting it, to be honest," I admit, chewing on my lip. "I thought I was going to die, and then he was there. I didn't realize I was wishing he would come until I saw him. That kiss—it was to save my life. Nothing else. He only kisses me to keep me alive or safe, not because he wants to."

"Um, wait. There has been more than one kiss?"

I cringe. I forgot I hadn't told her about the first kiss. "The other time didn't mean anything either."

"Sure, sure," she says, leaning against the wall, her eyes far too knowing. "You don't just kiss people, Calli. I've seen you take two males home and then immediately ditch them the next morning. Even then, you never kiss them for long. You don't let them close."

I stay silent because she is right. Nerelyth takes a new male home every weekend, and sometimes during the week, and she has had at least five long-term lovers. I've been running my entire life, and I don't know how to let anyone in, past my defenses I've had up for so long I can't remember a time before.

I'm sure, once, as a child, I let people in.

Now, I know they will either end up dead or they will leave me.

"Do you like him?"

I keep my tone cold. "He's a monster I'm working for. Nothing more."

The lie feels like acid on my tongue. He's different from what I thought he'd be, and he may look like a monster, but he doesn't act like it. Not to me. But he's still the king of the Wyerns, and I am a mortal. He has lived for hundreds of years, and he *will* live for hundreds of years, maybe even a couple of thousand if his race is like the fae, and my time in his life will be nothing more than a blip. I look at my friend, knowing it will be the same for her.

"You're a shit liar, Calli," she softly replies.

I clear my throat, and my voice is clipped. "The minute I find his sister, I'll probably never see him again, so all of it really doesn't matter, does it?"

"Calli," she reaches for my arm, and I move away, ignoring the hurt that flashes in her eyes.

"I need to find out who was on that ship today and what that magic was. I bet he was fae," I say. Work is normal. Work isn't going to break my heart.

Nerelyth nods. "I can look for you if you want?"

"Yes, please," I respond. "Look for a glowing orange sphere of magic and explosions. Big enough to explode a ship within seconds and set it on fire."

"Magic bomb of sorts, better than mortals can make," she muses, heading for the door. "You know where I am if you need a friend."

"I know," I reply softly, not looking at her as she leaves.

My stomach twists in knots, and I have to do something, anything else other than sit here thinking about Emerson. I've barely known him a week, and he has turned my life upside down. How is that even possible?

I shake my head and leave my office, heading up to the boss's room. When I get to the top of the stairs, I'm surprised to see the fae commander talking sharp and low with Merrick, who leans against the edge of the table with one leg crossed over the other. Both of the males swerve to look at me as I walk in, and I keep my head high as the fae commander's eyes run down me condescendingly.

Merrick nods at me. "This is Miss Sprite, one of my best enforcers. She was the one on the ship I've told you about."

I stop nearby and hold out my hand to the fae commander. He doesn't take it. "A pleasure to meet you, sir."

He looks down at me with nothing but contempt. Mostly for what my eyes give away. That somewhere, in my bloodline, a fae mixed with a lowly mortal. Something they never approve of. "Tell me what you know."

I clear my throat under the pressure of his gaze. "Hybrids jumped onto the ship, killing the captain of the port, and there was someone with them. Leading them. He made a sphere of orange magic in his gloved hands and ignored me for the most part. I jumped into the sea before the ship exploded."

The commander taps his foot on the ground. "What did you see of this person?"

"I think it was a fae male, sir."

The silence in the room becomes as thick as the humidity before a big storm. Fae. I don't expect it when the commander's hand whips out and slaps me hard against the cheek. I stumble a bit from the blow, pain lacing across my face, and I taste blood in my mouth.

Merrick is between us both within a second. "My staff are not to be hurt. She only speaks the truth."

"It is a disgrace to suggest an honorable fae would dare do this," he hisses at us as I straighten and move to Merrick's side, holding my head high. "I don't want to hear those dirty words coming out of your foolish mortal mouth again, or I will arrest you for crimes against the fae."

My insides go cold, and for a moment, I want to walk away and not help at all, but the brave and possibly foolish side of me keeps speaking. "Can you really account for the honor of every fae in the entire Ethereal City? That there's no possibility at all that someone would want to do this? Because I'm telling you, that was fae magic."

The commander takes a step towards me, but Merrick is quicker this time, blocking him completely from me with one step. "Do you want me to drag you back to the castle and throw you in the prisons there? Want to see how long you last with my guards? They do love pretty mortal girls."

Disgust rolls in my stomach. "Enough," Merrick sharply interrupts the fae commander's threat. "Miss Sprite means well, and we all want to find the prince, and we're just trying to help. Did he have any fae ex-lovers? Someone who might be angry at him? We all know that love can cause jealousy, and maybe someone has made a mistake they can't get out of."

The commander barks a laugh, looking away from me. "He is the sole heir of the fae. He has many, many ex-lovers. But he has one girlfriend who sticks with him through it all. She's been in near enough mourning since the kidnapping. Crying hysterically every day, so I've heard. I highly doubt if she did this, but I'll get her to speak to you."

"Thank you," Merrick replies, and I bite down on the inside of my cheek. The fae commander nods before he storms out of the room, and I run my finger across my cut lip, wiping away the blood.

Merrick turns to me, but I'm already stepping away. "Do you want something—"

"No, I'd just like to leave. Sir," I reply, my tone cold. I'm not mad at him, but I hate the fae, and I just want to leave.

My cheek is still stinging, burning, and I've cut the inside of my cheek worse than I thought. That was one hell of a hit from a supernatural, and I know I'm going to have a massive bruise for days, even with my faster than normal healing.

"You're dismissed. Have a good night, Miss Sprite."

I don't look back at him as I leave and grab my dirty washing in a bag before leaving. I stop off at a market stall for Flames and pull out a bunch of notes, a year's worth of money for some, and hand it to one of them. "Please take this to the family of Condan Sayers, and please don't tell them where it came from."

The Flame slips one note into his pocket before disappearing, and a slight weight is taken off my chest, knowing that one family will be okay until they can find work. I can't save them all, or help them all, but this time I can help just one. I catch a few people glancing my way, most likely at the swelling on my cheek, but no one says anything as I get back to my apartment building and head up the steps. I barely get three steps in my apartment before Emerson's form moves out of the shadows, and he walks to me, clicking on the lights.

Instantaneously, he goes still and his body tenses, icy magic trailing around the air in the room. For a second, I think I've done something wrong, and a trickle of fear goes down my spine as I take a step back. He storms over in three long strides, and his fingers catch my chin, gently tilting my head to the side to look at my bruised cheek.

"Who did this to you?"

I break away from him. "I don't need a monster in shining armor to protect me, Emerson. Leave it."

"No," he growls right back as I break away from him. I feel his magic follow me, brushing against my skin, and I spin around. "You can't heal it. People would know. My boss would ask why I don't have a bruise and cut lip. You've got to leave it."

He growls louder, but his magic ebbs away, and the room becomes a little warmer. His hands are still in fists, and he looks ready to break my apartment as I go to the icebox and grab a load of ice, wrapping it in one of my towels and holding it to my cheek and lip. I go sit on the sofa, lying down and closing my eyes.

I don't need to open them to feel him standing over me. His shadow does enough.

"Who did it, Doe? I want a name."

I sigh. "Why does it even matter?"

"It matters to me. Name. Now."

I snuggle into my worn cushion. "Will you let me sleep if I tell you?"

Emerson tucks a blanket over me, and I open my eyes, surprised as he leans over me. "Yes."

I search his eyes. "The commander of the fae. He didn't like my suggestion that it was a fae that blew up the ship."

Emerson's jaw tightens as he rises up, and he walks away. "Get some sleep, Doe. I'll be back soon."

I yawn, fighting off sleep. "Where are you going?"

"Sleep, Doe," he simply replies, and seconds later, I hear the door quietly shut behind him. I must be more tired than I thought, because within seconds, I fall asleep. I nearly jump when I hear the door opening, and I blink at the darkness in the room as I sit up, wincing at my cheek. It takes me a second to register that Emerson is back, and he is covered in blood.

"What did you do?" I whisper, my voice like a ghost. I raise my hand to my neck as he doesn't reply with anything other than a grunt and walks past me, straight into my bathroom. I climb up off the sofa and go after him. "You can't just come to my apartment, covered in blood, and not tell me anything."

Emerson's voice is empty of emotion. "I can."

I don't expect to see him near naked in the room, his ass on full display as he leans over to pull his boots off with his trousers bunched around his ankles. By the goddess, he has a perfect ass. My cheeks brighten as I quickly turn away and listen as he throws the rest of his clothes on the floor in my bathroom and flicks the shower on. After he has climbed into the shower behind the frosty glass partition, I look back. My breath hitches in my throat as I can still see him outlined behind the glass. His flawless, built and impressive body.

I gulp. "Where did you go?" I lean my hip against the counter and cross my arms when he doesn't answer. "I'm not going anywhere till you answer the question, because I've got a funny feeling you just did something really stupid."

"I didn't," he coldly replies.

"Was it something to do with the hybrids? Did you find a clue?"

He grunts a somewhat agreement, and I sigh. For a moment... I thought he might have... no, I'm being ridiculous. He wouldn't care that much. No one cares about me that much. Plus fae, especially the commander, can hit as many mortals as they like. There are no rules against fae hurting mortals like there are laws about mortals hurting fae.

"Are you going to watch me the entire time I shower, Doe?" he questions, a hint of amusement in his voice. "You are more than welcome to strip and join me."

I nearly choke on thin air as I stumble for the door. "I'm going to bed."

His laugh follows me out as my skin feels like it's on fire, and I embrace the cool air of my bedroom. I quickly get into my pajamas and climb into my bed, well aware there is little chance Emerson is going to sleep on the sofa or let me. Surprisingly, I don't have it in me to argue with him tonight.

Thankfully, he is wearing loose dark pants as he comes into the bedroom and takes my breath away. His hair is wet, beads of water dripping down his chest, and he looks so normal for a moment.

He climbs onto the bed, his wing tucking around me like a blanket, and I end up falling asleep far easier than I should in the arms of a monster.

CHAPTER
ELEVEN

The Wyern race are predominantly male born, with the occasional female, but any heir of a Wyern is blessed with the shifted form. The Wyern race was first recorded ten thousand years ago, drawn simply as winged males on stone walls found within Goldway City. There are many more records of Wyerns spread around the many cities of Wyvcelm but none more than the Forgotten Lands. Not much information is known on the Forgotten Lands as guests are not invited into the deep cavern cities and castles. When the great Wyern began, it was said to be started by the birth of a child who was to be king. Many of the Wyerns believed this child was prophesied to give his seed to the fae, and together they would rule the entire world. The fae and Wyerns came together to give this future a chance, but as records show, this only ended in the Wyern race banished from Ethereal City, Goldway City and Junepit City. The fae have condemned the race as monsters after The Great War that divided them from our world. The Wyern—

I barely get to sit down at my desk with my book before Wendy walks in, her heels clicking on the floor. "Fridays are always my favorite day."

I smile at her, leaning on my desk and closing the book on Wyerns I'd just started reading on the way over. Her eyes tighten as she looks at my cheek, but she doesn't question it. It's a fucked up job being an enforcer, and bruises are nothing new to us. "Really? I always had you down as a Monday person."

She laughs sweetly. "Mondays require a lot of energy to get out of bed. Here, I have something for you."

She passes me a note, and the expensive paper lets me know it's from the boss. "Did you hear what happened last night? To think we were one of the last ones to see him alive."

"What happened last night?" I ask, undoing the seal on the note, thinking of this morning. I woke up again to an empty apartment besides Posy. Louie came in moments later, and he was delighted to see the ridiculous amount of food laid out on the counter from Emerson. He cooked for me again. He saved my life, and I'm now worrying about him. The bastard is making me care, and I don't like it. It goes against every damn rule I have. Rules are there for a reason... to protect my heart. I'm so lost in thoughts of Emerson that it takes a few seconds for Wendy's words to hit home. "The commander of the fae was found dead last night. He was assassinated in his home."

The room becomes too small, too filled with every thought that slams into my mind over and over. The fae commander is dead?

Emerson coming back covered in blood after I told him what the fae commander did? It can't be a coincidence, but if he did that... he did it for me.

By the goddess.

Shock has me silent as Wendy rattles on, "Between this, the funerals for the fae killed by the hybrids, the captain of the port dead, and the news finally breaking that the Fae Prince has been kidnapped, the city feels on edge. Everyone is on edge."

I nod.

"Right, well, I'll leave you for the day, Calliophe," she says, letting herself out as I grip the note tightly in my hand, unable to even let it go as the shocking realization that I might have been right last night tries to sink in. There is a very good chance Emerson went and killed the fae commander for hitting me. It can't be true. He wouldn't have done that for me—we barely know each other. And every interaction between us so far is a mixture of frustration or desperation. I'm not someone he should kill for.

My mouth goes dry as I lean back in my chair, and I barely even notice Nerelyth until she slides onto the edge of my desk in a tight black skirt and loose green shirt tucked in. Her red hair looks like waves cascading down her shoulders, and she smells like she had a very good night with a fae male.

"Now that asshole commander is dead, do we still get paid if we find the prince?" she asks, and I finally lift my eyes to meet hers, as she finds the bruise and cut lip I'm sporting. "What the fuck happened to your face?"

I clear my throat, wondering if I should tell her the truth. If Emerson did this, I'm in deep shit. The Fae Queen will have me killed within a second, but this is Nerelyth, and she wouldn't tell a soul. I glance at the closed door to make sure it's shut. "The fae commander. He hit me last night, and I told Emerson. Emerson left and came back hours later, covered in blood. Blood that scented like fae."

Her eyes widen and we both stay silent for a moment. I see her ticking over everything. "No one knows who killed the commander, but he would have had plenty of enemies. This won't get back to you."

I blow out a breath. "That's not what I'm worried about. I don't know for certain Emerson did this, but if he did, why?"

"Because no male should ever raise a hand to a female? Because some males still have honor, and the commander fucking deserved it."

The venom in her voice is so unlike her normal voice that I can't help but smile, remembering the first time we met. She was so new and shiny, polished and perfect, and on our first mission we ended up covered in literal horse shit while searching for a Snake Kind male who killed his mate. Even covered in shit, she looked flawlessly perfect, and when we had caught him and sent him along with some other enforcers, we both looked at each other and laughed until our voices went.

I finally speak. "You're right—I've just never had anyone protect me like that. I never expected the monster who kidnapped me to be the first."

"The more you tell me of this Emerson, the less I believe he is a monster at all. The Wyerns are nothing like the history books tell us, are they?"

I shiver, unable to answer that one with the truth, not yet, and open the note. "Boss wants me to meet him at that posh restaurant tomorrow night. You know, the new one that recently opened near the far side of the city and everyone talks about?"

"Oh, the Graisfall. Why does he want you to meet him there?"

"Doesn't say. Just tells me to meet him

there at seven tomorrow night." I gnaw on my lip, knowing I'm meant to be at the Wyern castle tomorrow and all weekend, as per Emerson's demands, but the boss might have a lead. That, I can't miss. I have to find the princess and Fae Prince, because every day that passes means the chances of finding them alive are getting slimmer.

"I think he just wants to take you on a date at the most romantic restaurant in Ethereal City, bar what the fae have," she teases with a grin. "You have to wear something pretty."

"It's not a date," I glower.

"He's gorgeous, and so are you. You are both mortal and have a lot in common," she says like she is ticking off a well-thought-out list, and the problem is, she isn't wrong.

"He is also a bossy asshat," I mutter.

"One's trouble and one's not," she delicately says. "There are things in life that we run from and things we are attracted to that we shouldn't have. Especially males. It's okay to want Emerson, but we both know you will get hurt. You're close to him already. Anyone can see that."

Her words hit deep. "Sounds like you're

talking from experience."

"I've never seen you actually let anyone close to you, ever. You barely let me in, and I still don't know everything about your past, what really haunts you and what you hide from me. I'm your best friend and I've never once seen you off your game as much as you have been since you met the Wyern King."

I cross my arms. "Say it how it is, why don't you?"

She widens her arms. "Can't you see how dangerous this is? You're mortal, Calli, and being close to him will get you killed."

"It's just a job—"

"So we are lying to each other now?" she questions, arching an eyebrow. "In all the years I've known you, you act like anyone close is going to be pulled away from you like a toy. But not him, right? I know you, and I can see the difference anytime you mention him, and we both know he will break your heart."

I grit my teeth. "Because I'm just a mortal, right?"

"No. Supernaturals aren't like mortals, Calli. Love isn't really a thing for them unless it's their mate, and they will dump anyone for their mate. It's even worse for high-up supernaturals, those who are bound to marriages that aren't anything other than alliance and paperwork. He is a king and he will marry for that paperwork one day. You have a chance at a date tomorrow, with a mortal, and I think you should go. That's all I'm saying here."

"You know what, I've told you a lot about me over the years, despite how painful it is for me to talk about my past, but you've told me absolutely nothing. I don't know where you grew up or if you have family. I don't know who you are, really, and yet you're judging me right now?"

She huffs, her eyes flashing with pain. She slides off my desk in the graceful way that all sirens do and goes to the door, her back facing me and her shoulders tight. "I don't tell you anything in order to protect you. I'm always looking after you because I love you, and I don't want you to have a shit life chasing a supernatural who will never choose you."

"You don't have to protect me," I bite out.

She turns the handle. "Then I'm sorry. I'm going to carry on researching the fae magic."

When she shuts the door behind her, I drop

my head onto the desk and resist the urge to smack my head against it. I shouldn't have snapped at her like that. She was only looking out for me, even if I don't like the truth. She is right. She is so right. Having any feelings for Emerson is going to end with my heart being smashed and thrown to the wind. But treating tomorrow night like anything near a date is insane. Merrick has made it clear he just thinks I'm annoying. I need to say sorry to Nerelyth. I go to the door, pulling it open and stopping when I find Nerelyth and Wendy outside.

"Oh, you're here. There's been a Flame here, sent this from the boss. He says you both have permission to go and search the house where the Fae Prince was taken. There isn't much left to search, but he asks that you go anyway," she says, and I nod, looking at my friend, but she isn't looking my way at all.

Nerelyth nods. "Enchantments?"

"Banned in the fae district, I'm afraid," Wendy reminds her.

"Brilliant," I mutter, but Nerelyth is already walking to the door. I say goodbye to Wendy before jogging to catch up and stay at the same pace as her as we head out into the gloomy morning. Light rain constantly falls as we head to the fae district, a solid hour on foot, and by the time we have walked a good half of the way, we are soaked.

"I'm sorry," I tell Nerelyth as we walk past the nicer houses on the border.

She sighs. "Me too. Your personal life is none of my business. I'm just worried about you, and it didn't come out the way I intended."

"You're right to be worried. I'm a mess right now," I admit, biting on my lip. "Emerson has put me in a tailspin, and I needed you to smack me out of it. To remind me of the big picture."

"Anytime," she softly replies, offering me her pinkie finger. "Besties still?"

I link my pinkie finger with hers and grin. "Forever."

She wraps her arm around me and rests her head on my shoulder before she starts telling me about the fae male she is casually fucking for the week and how big his—

"Mortals and sirens are not welcome here. Get lost."

I pause in front of the fae guard, one of at

least twenty lined up outside the thick black walls that line the fae district. This guard is tall and looms over me with glowing blue eyes that stand out in his black leather armor lined with gold stripes. On his breastplate is the royal sigil —a perfect gold rose above a black compass. He is stunning in the way all fae are, and he might take my breath away, but I don't show it. I don't buckle in the sheer presence of this fae male.

"We are M.A.D. enforcers, and we have been invited to see the last place the Fae Prince was before he was kidnapped," Nerelyth coldly replies.

He sighs and looks over his shoulder. "Open the gate."

The gate silently swings open, and the guards step aside. The one who spoke to us looks at Nerelyth. "I will escort you. Do not speak to anyone, and keep your eyes to yourself."

I bite on my tongue rather than tell him to fuck himself as he walks away, and we are left with no other option than to follow. The first thing I notice when I step into the fae district is how it just smells better than anywhere else in

Ethereal City, and it is cleaner, too. From the shiny white stone path, the red, purple and green bushes that line the edges and plains of grass fields, it's like a fairy-tale version of the rest of the world. The homes are all white too, with a purple slate roof and framed windows, and tiny fence-lined gardens. My senses are overwhelmed, and it's just like I imagined it would be.

The air smells of flowers and sweetness like someone is baking cakes nearby, and it's magically warmer here. Fae children run past us, giggling together, and some wave at the guard, who ignores them. The fae children may ignore that we are here while they have fun, but the adults we come across do not. Every male or female fae turns their noses up or outright sneers in my direction like I'm a bad smell. We might all live in the same city, but it's like two different worlds.

Eventually everything, every perfect house, begins to look the same, and Nerelyth sneezes. "Damn flowers."

I try not to chuckle as she has a point. There are flowers everywhere, and roses seem to be a fan favorite of the fae, most likely in honor of the royal family. They are too expensive for most, and not many in the poor district, or even where I live, are going to honor the Fae Queen when they spend their lives suffering under her rule. No wonder she never leaves this district. It would be like her taking off her imaginary rose-tinted glasses.

The guard leads us to what is left of a house, and it stands out like a fish flopping on land. One half of the house is completely caved in, the other is missing a roof, and bricks are scattered everywhere. In front of the house are thousands of flowers in patterns, teddy bears and letters pinned to what is left of the fence. Several houses around this one look the same, and my eyes focus on a house nearby with hybrid claws scratched down the stone before I look back. "Here you go, but I'm sure you lot will be as useless as everyone that has come here."

Nerelyth and I look at each other, and I roll my eyes as I walk past the useless ass guard.

The black front door is held open by a rock, and what once was probably an exquisite little garden is nothing more than smashed flowers and rocks. We head inside through the door, and I sigh. Everything is covered in rubble and dust or torn to pieces.

There are only three surviving rooms to really look at, and they are empty of anything useful. This is a dead end.

"I'm going to check the back of the house," Nerelyth says, and I nod, leaving her to it. We both know there is nothing to find here. I feel something flickering in the pocket of my coat, and I pull it out. It's the compass I took from the ship, and it's spinning like crazy. Yet it didn't spin anywhere else but when I was on that ship. I stare at the spinning dial, wondering if it could be something or nothing before shoving it back in my pocket and heading out to find Nerelyth. I find her at the back of the house, looking at dried blood splattered against the wall.

"Something tells me they let us here to please the boss."

"I agree. We should go."

She nods, walking with me back to the guard. "I'll pop over with a dress. Date or not, you need to look good, and that is a job for your bestie."

I grin at her. "I'm all yours, Nerry."

CHAPTER
TWELVE

"Just me," I shout out as I use my shoulder to push the front door open while reading the newspaper with a massive painting print of the Fae Prince on the front page. The Fae Prince is a beautifully alluring pretty boy. There is no doubt about it, but something about his blue eyes seems colder than a winter storm. I close the newspaper and shut the door behind me.

"I'm afraid your friend is hiding," a gentle female voice replies.

Smiling, I put my newspaper, my borrowed dress, and my bag down before taking off my coat. "I wouldn't call us friends."

She softly laughs as I walk into the living

area and lean against the cabinet, surprised to see the fae female on my couch. Zurine looks extremely out of place, like a diamond in the trash, as she elegantly perches on my crappy sofa. She has a silver blouse tucked into black trousers, and her enchanting silver hair is wrapped into a tight bun. Sparkling diamond earrings hang from her ears. "You're brave to wear earrings like that around here."

She smiles fondly at me, but there is power in her voice. "I've been trained and crafted into a weapon since my birth. Mortals wouldn't stand a chance."

"Good to know," I reply. "I wasn't expecting you here."

She shrugs a shoulder. "You knew one of the court would come to stay. Thank you for having me. You have a very nice apartment."

I snort. "I do not." She tries not to smile and fails. "Have you eaten? I can cook something for you, as I ate at work with a friend."

"No, thank you. I've eaten already," she casually replies. "How is everything going since we last spoke?"

My chest lurches. "We're getting closer."

"Hmm," she replies. "We are all worried.

The longer Solandis is missing, the more risk there is for her not to come back alive at all. Many Wyerns are calling for war and blaming the fae."

My insides turn like a storm. "Would Emerson let that happen?"

She places her hands on her knee. "He is working hard to calm the masses. They listen to him, but there is still a royal missing."

I blow out a breath. "Truthfully, we are being watched by someone. Someone fae."

She tilts her head to the side. "What do you mean?"

I tell her about the ship and the hooded male with the hybrids. "I've not heard of fae power like that," she tells me.

My shoulders deflate. Dammit. "My partner is researching it, but so far, we haven't found much."

"I will make my own research into family bloodlines," she informs me. "Anything else I can help with?"

"Nope," I reply with a tired smile. "Oh, but I guess I should tell you. I can't come to the court tomorrow for the weekend like agreed."

She goes still. "Why not?"

"I can't come to the Wyern castle—I mean, what do you even call it?"

Zurine straightens her back. "The Wyern Castle is fine, but some older Wyerns call it The Oblitus Castle. The entire castle is dedicated to the royal court, and the families live in the courts, along with the king and his family, of course. You won't find anyone in the castle that isn't in the court or a personally chosen and trained guard."

"Except the mortal females," I point out.

She chuckles. "Yes, but I do try to pretend they aren't there. All of them except you."

"Are you dating one of the Wyerns?" I curiously ask.

She looks away. "No, it isn't like that for me," she says with an iciness I've never heard her use.

"I'm sorry, I shouldn't—"

She clears her throat. "No, my reaction was uncalled for. It's natural for you to ask questions. So yes, please call my home the Wyern Castle. The rest of the city has a different name, but we're not allowed to tell you unless you join our court. As an outsider, I mean."

"I'll just keep imagining the rest of the city is as impressive as the castle," I reply.

"It's certainly something extraordinary and deserves the protection of our king," she replies, her eyes filled with light for a moment.

I leave her to grab a drink from the kitchen and find a freshly made pint of orange juice. After pouring myself a glass, admiring how I get to drink this now, I go back to Zurine. "You never did tell me what a fae female is doing in a Wyern court."

"We've met twice," she hardily laughs. "And you always ask exactly what you're thinking, don't you? I'm not sure if you are brave or foolish."

"A bit of both is your best guess, I've found," I reply with a grin.

"I like you, either way, Calliophe," she fondly replies. "You remind me of myself when I was younger. I asked too many questions, too."

"Find any questions you didn't want the answers to?"

"Too many," she quickly replies, a sting to her words. She brushes up some stray dust off her knee. "I've been in the Wyern court for nearly a hundred years. I spent the previous two hundred years of my life in the fae inner court."

My eyes widen. "The actual inner court of the queen?"

"Yes," she replies tightly. "My parents, well, I was born to that life. I knew the Fae Prince's parents well. I was heartbroken by the news of their death."

"Fae sickness is horrible. I nearly died myself from it," I admit, shivering at even the memory of that terrible illness. I remember thinking if the fae princess and her mate couldn't be saved, then there was no hope for me. "I'm sorry."

"I'm glad you survived. That mortal blood of yours is lucky," she replies. "I've not known the sickness, thank the goddess."

"So you know the prince?"

"No," she replies. "He was born after I left and came to the Wyern court. But his mother and father were the kindest fae I've ever known. I wish they didn't die the way they did, and I wish more that my circumstances meant I could have held their hands at least once before they left this world."

"Why do you say they were kind?"

She smiles to herself. "Have you ever known two people drawn to each other from the second they met? It's like watching two shooting stars blast across the night sky, knocking everything and anything out of their way to get to each other. They loved each other deeply, well before they found out they were true mates."

"I didn't know they were true mates."

She shrugs a shoulder. "It's rare that a royal finds a true mate in a high ranking fae that she can actually marry. They don't advertise it, because they believe in only marrying their heirs off to connect bloodlines and increase power. My parents were together for that reason."

"Why'd you leave?"

"I feel like I'm being interrogated now." She arches a perfect eyebrow.

"You're not. You don't have to answer," I softly reply. "I'm just more curious than a cat."

"Well, we've only just met, and I don't know if you'll sell my story to whoever will pay the most to publish it," she carefully replies.

I try not to take it personally. "You don't know me, but I won't tell anybody."

"But you are in this for money, and anybody who needs money as desperately as you cannot be trusted."

It's a blunt and honest answer. "It's your past. You don't have to share it with me for us to be friends."

"I don't have many female friends," she muses. "As you might have noticed, the royal Wyern court is made up of male warriors."

"Someone should change that," I suggest.

She laughs. "I was hoping Solandis would take a seat at the court one day. When her ideals are less…"

"Rebellious?"

"Ah, Lorz has been talking. He can never keep a secret," she replies with amusement in her eyes.

"So, back to the subject. Do you think the Fae Prince is like his parents in nature?"

Her lips fold into a thin line. "All I will say is from rumors and accounts, the prince is not like his parents, who were good and kind. He has been brought up in the shadow of the queen, and you should be very wary when you do find him. He will sooner kill and torture a mortal than admit one saved his ass."

Noted.

"Why do you think he was taken? Your personal opinion, I mean."

She looks over out of the tiny window. She can see nothing more than the night ahead of her and the glittering stars. "I think we're all on the brink of a war, and we always have been. There isn't peace in Wyvcelm anymore. The siren and the fae alliance is crippled and precarious at best and written on old texts that are thousands of years old. They were written when the queen was a bright, young new queen, and she wasn't mad as they say she is now. When madness stirs in the leaders of the world, the rest of us should be frightened."

I shiver, goose bumps flittering up my arms. "We have been at peace for over a thousand years."

"A peace made on a lie," she quietly replies and turns to look right at me with her purple and blue eyes, a swirling mix of paint. "And lies always come out in the end. When you find the missing royals, Calliophe, take the money and your ward, and get as far away from Ethereal

City as you can. Don't look back, don't contact anyone here. Mortals are nothing in war."

"Thanks for the advice," I reply.

The conversation goes dry, and it feels awkward as we both don't look at each other. I actually want Posy to stop eavesdropping and come out here to make it less awkward. I'm thankful when Zurine speaks first. "As for you, why can't you come to the castle tomorrow?"

"Oh, right," I say. "My boss has asked me to come with him to a restaurant. I have to meet him there at seven at night, but I can come after I'm done."

"A date?"

"No. My boss isn't like that, not with me, anyway. There's got to be a reason why he wants us there. Last time, he took me to the port, and that was the best clue I've had. We were close to nearly finding out who had done this. I felt it."

"Is he a good-looking mortal?" she questions. "It could be a date and a mission."

I laugh. "He is stunning for a mortal. Many suspect he is inches off being a supernatural himself, but it's not a date. Although my best friend seems to think otherwise."

"Your friend is likely right. You are very beautiful, Calliophe, and any male would jump at a chance for a date."

I blush under her compliment, but it's not true, not when compared to her; I'm the ugly duckling in a pack of swans. "I don't date."

"Why not?" she asks, sounding genuinely curious.

I don't know why I tell her the truth. "Because dating is a risk of catching feelings for someone."

"Feelings between two souls are to be treasured and chased," she kindly replies. "Not feared."

"I'm happy with how my life is, thank you. I don't need a male in my life to control me and make me love them, only to lose them," I tightly say. "I'm better alone."

"I hate to tell you that living a life without letting anyone in is only being cruel to yourself. You haven't been alive until you've fallen in love. Even if your heart is broken in the end, you lived. You breathed life. Don't shut yourself away for the rest of your short mortal life. Live it."

I take her words in, but they're not going to

lower the icy walls that I placed around my heart. They are there for a reason, because when I lose someone, it crushes me. It devastates me, and there's been times in the past when a foster parent died where I just wanted to give up on life. I've thought about it too many times, been hurt too many times to open up myself to that again. I can't.

Emerson flickers through my mind, and I swat that thought away.

By the goddess, I shouldn't be thinking of him.

I'm so lost in my thoughts that I don't catch the sound of my door handle until just as my door opens and Louie walks in, coming to a quick stop. His eyes go wide as he takes in the fae female on the couch, and he slowly looks at me. "Shut the door, Louie."

He looks in a shocked trance as he shuts the door and stays near it. "Zurine, this is Louie. Louie, this is my friend Zurine."

Zurine stands up and walks over to him. But to my surprise, she kneels down and offers him her hand. He very carefully shakes it like he's scared he might break her.

"N-n-nice to meet you," he says, stumbling over his words.

Zurine pretends not to notice. "It's a pleasure. Calliophe has told me how fond of you she is. You are lucky to have her."

"I am," he replies, looking at me. "She is my sister. Not in blood, but I don't care."

I wink at him, my heart warming as Zurine rises. "You are an honorable male, Louie. You can now say you have a fae friend."

"Really?" he replies, puffing up his chest. "That would be so cool. My friends will never believe me, though."

She chuckles and I walk over, ruffling his hair. "Are you hungry?"

"Yes," he groans, patting his stomach. "I had extra homework today because Mr. Blieue decided we didn't do enough last week, and I've just finished it. It was boring anyway."

"There are loads of leftovers in the icebox," I instruct him. *Loads* is an understatement because Emerson's massive breakfasts and lunches he leaves out could feed an army. "Eat away."

I help Louie get a plate as he decides between the food left, taking a little of everything. I smile at him, happy to see him eating like he should. There have been too many times when we have had scraps for dinner, and worse times when it's been a choice between him and me eating that night, and I've forced him to eat.

"You love him dearly. You might not date, but you have people around you'd fight for just as fiercely. You are a contradiction, Calliophe."

I don't look back at Zurine. "He's as close to family as I'm ever going to get, and there isn't anything I wouldn't do for him. You're right... but falling in love with someone is different. Love is nothing but dangerous."

"You can't help who you love," she softly replies. "As for Louie, I respect your choice to mark him as your ward. Your family."

"But fae don't do that, do they?"

She quietly laughs. "No. Fae protect their bloodlines, and there are no wards. If you find yourself without family, you are married off. No matter the age. Bloodlines are honored in the fae, and it's all they care about. Blood is power."

"I heard a rumor once that nearly all the

powerful fae bloodlines have died out, beside the royal bloodline."

"You heard correctly, but I wouldn't speak that out loud. Many wish the queen had more children so that the Fae Prince wasn't the only heir to the throne left. Others want him wed and producing an heir quickly. If he is dead, there isn't another fae bloodline powerful enough to take over. Not left anyway. There were once three powerful bloodlines who fought over the throne."

"What happened to them?"

"It doesn't matter. They are dead. Loyalty doesn't come from blood," she quietly says. "I've learned what you have. Emerson saved my life, and Lorenzo taught me how to live it. I will be in their debt forever."

We spend the next hour with Louie, who doesn't once look away from Zurine, like if he blinks, she might disappear. Eventually I put my hand on his shoulder, stopping him mid-conversation about how the science department at school smells like perfume due to the teacher wearing too much. "Isn't it time for you to go to bed?"

He rolls his eyes at me. "There is no school tomorrow, remember?"

"But I'm tired, Louie. It's best we all get some sleep," Zurine suggests.

"Okay," he quickly replies.

I try not to roll my eyes.

"Remember, I'm not here most of this weekend. Could you check on Posy?"

"Sure." He grimaces, and I don't blame him. "See you on Monday, Calli. Bye, Zurine."

"Bye, Louie," Zurine says, waving at him as he goes to the door. He looks back at her once before going out of it and shutting it behind him. I get up and lock the door before cleaning up after his dinner.

"Right, it's been one hell of a day, and I need some sleep," I admit around a yawn.

She stands. "I hope I'm not being rude, but would you like me to heal your face from that bruise? How did you do it, anyway?"

"No, thank you," I blurt. "Emerson already tried to heal me, but I refused him because people will notice. My boss would notice if the bruise was gone. Plus, it barely hurts anymore."

"He what?"

I look back, surprised to see her looking completely shocked. "He tried to heal you? King Emerson?"

"Yes," I say with a scrunch of my nose. "Actually, he did heal me once when he saved me from drowning the other day. I kinda wish I had his powers. It would make it much easier in my job."

She is silent for such a long time. I'm unsure what to say or why she is so bothered by Emerson healing me. She eventually blinks herself out of it and looks down at the sofa, rubbing her arm. The sofa is in a sorry state, thanks to Lorenzo and Emerson sitting on it with their heavy, muscular bodies and massive wings.

"You know what? You can sleep in my bed if you want? I promise I don't snore."

She smiles widely. "I would appreciate that. I do not snore either."

"That isn't a surprise. You're too perfect to snore."

She chuckles and heads to the bathroom with a silk bag she picks up off the side.

I head to my room and get changed, using the bathroom after she comes out in silver pajamas and climbs into my bed. My room still scents like Emerson, and I wonder if she is going to ask if Emerson slept in here, as I get into the bed on the other side of where I usually sleep. I'm too tired to ask Zurine to move over.

I click my fingers, and the light turns off, and I close my eyes. "By the way, why are you always wearing silver?"

Her voice is softer than my sheets and fills the air like the sweet smell of flowers. "Silver reminds me of blades and ice. It reminds me I'm strong."

I don't have the courage to ask her why she needs to be reminded of her strength. Strength now only reminds me of one person, not a color, but if he could be defined by a color, it would be the magenta purple that stretches across the sky before the sun sets and darkness rules the world.

CHAPTER
THIRTEEN

I stare at myself in the tall glass windows of the busy restaurant, mortals flittering around me and a few looking my way. Blue light casts a halo over my body from the flickering restaurant sign above me, lit up with magic and glittering against the dark night. Just for a moment, I hardly recognize myself in my reflection, because I look better than I ever have. It's not just the dress Nerelyth chose for me from her excessive wardrobe collection, but the thinness I had to my cheeks is gone, and my skin glows warmly as I'm actually getting some sleep at the moment. My eyes are brighter than the light pink dress I'm wearing, which fits me like a glove from my shoulders down to my knees. There is a long slit that goes all the way up to the top of my thigh, making it easy to walk, and the back of the dress rises all the way to my neck, a dragon pattern in lace. My hair is up, messily held with a few sharp dagger slides, and with them, I only have two other weapons on me, daggers pushing into the base of my heels.

Still, I feel like I'm not wearing enough weapons for this night, and I'm not sure what to expect. Nerelyth's words whisper in my ear like a betraying thought. A date. This could be a real date.

I push down on the pressure rising in my chest at the thought, not letting it swallow me whole, and smile tightly as I walk to the entrance doors, held open with velvet rope.

The salty sea breeze brushes over my skin like a whisper of a kiss, and I straighten my back. "May I serve you, madam?"

I almost flinch, not hearing or seeing the siren woman until she is standing in front of me. Her uniform is all blue, matching the tones of the outside of the restaurant, and her smile is as warm as her seawater eyes. "I'm here with Merrick Night."

"Ah," she replies, tucking her dark hair behind her ear and inclining her head to the side for me to follow. "He has been waiting."

"I'm usually late for things. Okay, I'm always running late," I inform her with a playful smile.

She looks back at me, her night-kissed skin glittering like diamonds in the light. "Males should wait for their females. It keeps them on their toes."

I wink at her, chuckling softly. She reminds me of Nerelyth, and for a moment, I wonder if she knows my friend and any of her many secrets. I look behind me as I head inside, searching the empty street and the fae lights to spot any wings hiding in the darkness. I don't find any, but it doesn't mean I'm not being watched. It's been a long day, and Zurine hasn't left my side for any of it. I got the suspicion she didn't want to go and tell Emerson that I wasn't coming back with her tonight and I'll come back later. I'm not sure he's going to take that well that I'm breaking out of our agreement on the first weekend. I've only known him for a short time, but I suspect there will be a Wyern temper tantrum going on back there. I will need a few drinks before I face that.

I should fear the Wyern King having a temper tantrum. Should. Some part of me doesn't, and that part of me is stupid.

I shake my head at myself and walk further in, down a dimly lit tunnel and through to the central part of the restaurant, but I don't look at any of it. I only see Merrick waiting for me, his arms crossed, and I forgot how stunning he is until this moment. He doesn't have the alluring beauty like Emerson, or the raw magnetic power, but for a mortal, Merrick is something else. Tonight he looks so much less like my boss and so much more like someone I would take home for fun. For a night.

His lips part open when I walk up to him, almost in shock, and I take a second to admire the expensive tux that fits to his body perfectly. His dark hair is brushed to the side, and his grey eyes lock onto mine as I stop in front of him. "Good evening, boss."

"Tonight, Miss Sprite, my name is Merrick."

I tilt my head to the side. "Merrick."

He smiles and uncrosses his arms. "You look bewitching, Miss Sprite."

The restaurant, the siren nearby, everything fades away until I can't see anything but his eyes searching mine and the fact I don't know how to reply. I feel heat creeping up my neck as he looks me over once more before offering me his arm. "Have I rendered you speechless, Miss Sprite?"

I snap out of it and slide my arm through his and let him lead me up the steps, giving me a full view of the entire place. I can see why everyone wants to go here. The restaurant is gorgeous, unique and magical. The restaurant floor is pitch black, and steel steps wrap around in circles, spreading up several levels. Stepping stones lead to floating tables, which float in the air in circles, and the black tables are even shaped like stars. While I'm on the bottom floor, I can see it is made to look like the night sky. There's not a table empty as the siren leads us up the stairs until we're nearly at the top row, and the drop is daunting as I look down once. I feel like I'm going to fall as I follow Merrick across the stepping stones, which are also shaped like stars. I feel a little more stable on my heels when I'm near the black table, which has a row of purple candles and fresh flowers as a centerpiece. It's a cozy table, with only two seats, and I feel Merrick's gaze on me as he pulls out a chair. I sit down as he goes around the table and takes the other seat.

The siren bows and leaves us, and a bottle of wine magically appears on the table along with two glasses. "The house wine. I chose before you came. I hope that's alright?"

"Perfect," I say as he picks the bottle up and pours us both a glass. I sip on the fruity wine as I keep looking around, marking the easy exits on instinct.

"You look so out of place, Miss Sprite."

I turn back to Merrick, a wall going up between us in my mind. "Expensive restaurants aren't a regular thing for me."

He sighs. "I didn't mean—excuse me. I meant you look uncomfortable. Is it the height?"

"It's not the height," I admit, gnawing on my bottom lip. I don't dare tell him I've had to get used to heights extremely fast because of the Wyerns. "Why are we here, Merrick?"

He leans back. "You've been distracted at work. I've noticed."

My heart races. "There are high stakes at the moment. I want to find the prince."

And princess.

Merrick swirls his wine. "Why do you give all your money to the boy and his mother's care?"

"So you know," I ask, not really a question at all.

He nods. "They aren't your biological family, so I'm curious."

I take another long sip. "Family isn't blood for me. Which is a good thing, considering I have no relatives. Louie and his mom are the closest I have. Even if they weren't, I couldn't let them suffer when I can help."

"There aren't many selfless people around these days," he counters.

"Doesn't mean I shouldn't be one of them. No matter what it costs me."

He takes a long drink. "You should have come to me. I would have helped you. I mean, I will help you if you'll let me."

My heart races. If he had asked me this a few weeks ago, I would have said yes. Screw my pride. I would have jumped at the chance to have anyone help me. But now... I don't need his help, and letting anyone like him close to me at the moment would risk my new circumstances being found out. "I'm good, thank you."

"Stubborn," he mutters with a frown.

"Did you bring me here to offer your help?" I ask, putting my glass down. "A meeting at the office would have been cheaper."

He laughs. "No, I brought you here for a reason."

"Go on," I say, leaning closer.

He lowers his voice. "Do you know the history of this restaurant?"

"I know nothing much about it," I admit, knowing I should have done some research instead of getting lost in reading the Wyern history book and the old fae symbol books. Both of which didn't offer me much useful information today. Zurine told me she could tell me more truthful information than the books before she made us both lunch.

He smiles, like he knows I wouldn't have done any research. "It's owned by the captain of the port's only brother, and until a year ago, he had no money. He'd always dreamed of opening this place, from my sources, and then suddenly he was given all the money he needed. Overnight. Claimed his brother gave him it."

I incline my head. "Where would the captain of the port get that kind of money?"

"That's the question, isn't it? I also found out he was given more money six months ago as this place was struggling to be finished and he'd spent all the money he had. Of course, he soon ran out of that money, and then he was given a shit ton of money once more."

"Is there any connection to the missing mortals on the ship?"

"Three ships have gone missing, Miss Sprite. The captain of the port hid the other two but didn't do a good job hiding the third. Every time his brother got money, a few days later, a ship full of mortals went missing."

"Fuck," I mutter.

"Indeed, Miss Sprite," he coolly replies. "I believe the captain of the port contacted whoever blew up that ship. I also believe his brother knows who it is. I have all the evidence needed to take him in, but I want to talk to him alone, outside the enforcer building. I don't trust anyone else to be here."

"Thank you, boss," I say.

"Merrick," he reminds me with an amused grin. "We are undercover, after all."

My lips tilt up. Loving Merrick would be so easy when he is nice like this, like slipping into a warm sea and letting it swallow you whole until there was nothing left. But I know he isn't always nice, and if I did fall for him, I'd end up killing him for being his usual asshole self.

"So to make conversation—"

I pause as a waiter comes to our table, and we both order our food before he walks away. "You were saying?"

I lean back in my seat. "Is it true you are friends with the Fae Queen?"

If he is surprised by my question, he doesn't show it. "Anyone that is friends with the Fae Queen wouldn't speak about that connection out here."

"I'll take that as a yes," I reply with a smile. "How about the rumors you hunted a pack of monsters down on your own and saved many fae lives?"

"Will you stop asking questions about my

past if I tell you one thing about my past?"

"Sure," I agree.

"Yes, I did hunt down a pack of monsters. There were seven of them, all fae turned monsters, and they took five female fae to breed and destroy. I saved them, what was left anyway, but their minds were shattered beyond repair. I don't talk about it because I felt I didn't save them quick enough or save anyone at all. They were and are broken."

We both go silent, and I try to catch his eyes, a grey storm brewing within them. "I'm sure, even broken and lost, through the cracks, they are thankful you stopped it. You saved them, and maybe one day they can recover."

His voice is flat. "They won't."

Neither of us says a word for a long time, and I'm regretting asking anything by the time the food arrives and we silently begin to eat. After a few delicious mouthfuls of the fish, I know I can't come here again, or I'd be addicted to eating this. It's amazing. Merrick's voice nearly makes me jump. "The owner, Maurt, is now one of the richest males in the city outside of the fae, and getting him alone was impossible until tonight. He is having a meeting here in an hour with some of the pirates that knew his brother well. A farewell meal in respect."

"So we will have a chance to get him alone," I say. "Even if it's in a restroom or something."

"I'd prefer to make sure he can't leave his office," Merrick smoothly says. "He is known to be a weak male. We will use that against him."

The cold efficiency in his voice almost makes me feel bad for Maurt. Almost. Considering he likely sold hundreds of mortals to be turned into hybrids and killed.

"I wanted this to be a date."

I pause and lower my fork back onto the plate. His grey eyes are on me. "Not just work."

I stumble for words. "What?"

He places his elbows on the table and leans closer, his leg brushing mine. "I've wanted to ask you out for a long time, Miss Sprite, but I'm your boss. This was as close as I'm allowed."

"You're my boss. I've rarely even heard you call me by my first name, and I thought I constantly irritated you," I blurt.

"I shall call you Calliophe more often?" he suggests, his voice dark and luring. I swear I can smell smoke in the air. "And yes, you irritate me, but in the best way. I don't want that to stop."

"I don't date," I tell him, my words too quick.

His eyes narrow. "Is there a male I'm not aware of?"

"No," I say with a hollow laugh, although my betraying heart thinks of one person. "I just don't—"

I pause mid-sentence when I hear a rattling female scream echo around us, and I stand up from the table, Merrick moving with me. We both look down to see half the restaurant on fire, massive orange and red flames crawling across the wall and floor, as people run out of the door. Right before a hybrid lunges across the room, grabbing onto the edge of one of the stars and pulling it down, knocking the table and everything off it, including the people who scream as they fall.

"Don't hesitate, Miss Sprite," Merrick commands, grabbing two swords out from a hidden space in the back of his tux, and the silver metal shines in the light. I pull out my daggers from my heels and kick them off, watching in horror as dozens of hybrids start flooding the room. I look up to see a family on a star above me, two young children held in their parents' arms. Merrick catches my eyes. "Evacuate, I'll distract."

I nod before running across the stones and up the steps, barely glancing back to see Merrick jumping across the star platforms and down to the hybrids. I look up, finding at least ten more people rushing down the steps to me. "I'm an enforcer. Stay behind me and run when you can get to the door. Okay?"

The children cry, but most of the adults nod in agreement. I make my way down the steps first, pausing to help a female from under a table and getting her to follow me down the steps. When I get to the third star down, a hybrid jumps into my path and growls at me.

"Hello, any chance you want to talk this out?" I suggest, bracing myself. Behind the hybrid, the stairs lead right to a clear space and an open door. I purse my lips as two more hybrids climb up the steps behind it. I look back at the scared people huddled together behind me. "Run when it's clear."

A few of them nod as I turn back, and I do

something extremely stupid. I run and jump straight into the hybrid, using its weight to smack into the other two, and all four of us crash off the steps and into the air. A cry stays locked in my throat as I slam my dagger into its neck, black blood coating my hands and neck as we both fall down. We land in a smack, the hybrid taking most of the brunt of the fall, and everything hurts as I climb off its dead body only to be grabbed by another hybrid monster. Its claws latch around my waist, and I twist, cutting through the arm with my dagger. The monster hybrid screams at me, the sound too mortal, as it stumbles away, and I look up to see Merrick effortlessly cutting through the hybrids one after another, a flash of silver in the darkness. I rush to his side, and he throws a sword in the air for me to catch, and I jump, using a fallen chair to catch it and bring it down over a hybrid's head.

"Go find the office, Sprite! The owner is in danger!" Merrick shouts at me as I pull my sword out and look around, finding the door to the back rooms with dead guards outside in pieces. People are flooding into the back exit doors, and I pause for a moment to watch the last of them get outside safely before ducking in through the door that says Staff.

There are three doors in here on one long corridor, and the fae lights are blinking on and off every second, making it hard to see much. The middle of the three doors slams open, and I clutch my sword as a familiar hooded male pauses in the doorway.

A gold sword, glittering with red blood, hangs from his tanned hand, and he tilts his head to the side as he watches me. "You're fae. Why are you doing this?"

Magic floods the corridor, and it takes me a second to realize he isn't attacking me but making sure I can't get to him. I touch an invisible wall of magic, and it burns my hand. I hiss and lower my hand, watching the hooded male. "You killed the owner. To cover your tracks, I bet."

"Smart mortals end up in watery graves," he replies, his voice deep. A trickle of fear crawls down my spine as I feel his magic brushing against me, like it's tasting me. "If you know what's good for you, stop."

"No," I snap. "Not when you're killing my people. Where are the princess and prince?"

His laugh is like bricks slamming into a window. "This is only going to end badly for you, Calliophe Sprite. Run while you still can. There won't be another chance."

I don't run, I don't move, and I swear he laughs before his magic literally explodes. I scream as I fly in the air and slam against the wall, hard enough to see black dots before my eyes. When my vision clears and I manage to stand up, I'm not surprised to see the hooded male is gone. How in the goddess did he know my name?

I stumble into the office room, not surprised to see a male lying, his body broken and his dark green hair like a bed of seaweed around his head, on the floor. My eyes widen when I see his chest move, and I rush across the office, falling to my knees at his side. His bright green eyes open and look up at me as he grabs for my hand, blood pouring from his wet lips. "C—om—pass."

The light leaves his eyes as the garbled word reaches my ears, and I let his hand drop. As I go to open a window to let his soul leave, I know we have one more clue, and it's in my apartment. The compass.

CHAPTER
FOURTEEN

The wall in my bedroom begins to shimmer right before I scent the magic in the air, spreading through the air around me. Posy is hanging off my headboard as I turn to her, tying my boots up. "Louie is going to come over and feed you. Please don't be mean."

Posy all but snorts. "Mean? Me? Never."

I roll my eyes and go back to tying my boots as the magic spreads around the room like the spray of snow before a winter storm. I sit on the edge of my bed as the wall begins to ripple like water on a lake right before shining like glass. Lorenzo steps right out of the wall and into my bedroom with a smug grin. His hair is messy, and there is a glaze to his eyes that suggests he has been having a good night with booze. There is a wicked light to his eyes that reminds me of his brother.

"There is my favorite girl," he coos.

"You're such a flirt," I glower.

"Not you." He clicks his tongue, walking around me and straight to Posy, who flies to his shoulder. He strokes the back of her neck, and she downright purrs. "How's the boring city treating you, sweetness?"

Posy basically purrs, and for a moment, I wonder if I should give them my room. "I don't leave this place, so I don't know."

"You make it sound like a jail," I mutter.

"For me, it is," she snaps before brushing her head against Lorenzo's cheek. "Come back soon if you get bored with her. Which you will."

"A pleasure, as always," he softly replies as she jumps off his shoulder and flies out of my room. Lorenzo's eyes flicker to the still healing claw marks on my arm from the hybrid earlier. I grab my waist-length, black, soft leather jacket off my bed and pull it on to cover them up, and continue getting dressed. Lorenzo is leaning against my dresser, poking my teddy bear's cheek when I'm done. "Interesting night, mortal?"

"Something like that."

Frustrating would be the better word for tonight. If we had just gotten to the owner sooner, we might have a real clue, other than a compass. Two mortals died, and many more were injured, but most were thankful to Merrick and me for getting them out. I left Merrick dealing with everything and lied, saying I needed to get back to Louie. It's on the tip of my tongue to ask Lorenzo if he knows anything about compasses and fae, when he straightens and walks near the wall, but I don't ask. This is my job, and it's likely he won't know anything about it either. He isn't fae. "Did you miss me?"

His tone is completely serious, but his eyes sparkle with humor as I walk to his side. "Nope. You Wyern lot are just as annoying as my bat roommate."

He laughs and I run my eyes over his leathers, tight against his body. "Aren't you warm?"

Lorenzo follows my gaze. "No, and even if I

was, I wouldn't take them off while in this city. The leather was designed by ancient witches as a gift to my father and his armies. They are as impenetrable as the goddess's sword. Nothing can cut through it."

The goddess's sword. I haven't heard that myth in a long time. A sword forged in the stars, said to be wielded by the goddess herself as she cut the world into existence and used the elements to breathe life into the land she made exist.

"Which means you only have to look out for your neck then."

Lorenzo looks down at me, his eyes like the bright leaves of the ancient forest surrounding the back of the city edges. "Don't go telling everyone our weakness, eh?"

"I'll try," I say with a smile.

"You're deflecting, mortal. How was your night?" he questions again. "In fact, don't tell me. Emerson wants to know, and he is in a foul mood. You caused it, you fix it."

"I'm not—"

"You are," Lorenzo replies. "And I'm going to get drunk and fuck a pretty mortal or two while you do. It's been a long day."

I cringe. "You're gross."

Lorenzo laughs and offers me his hand. "Don't get jealous now. There is plenty of me to go around."

"I'm sure you've been around plenty enough for all of Wyvcelm."

His laugh seems to light up the room, and I can't help but smile as I take his hand, which is warm and firm within mine. We step through the wall, and I instinctively tense up as the magic washes over me like warm water right before we come out into the room of mirrors. This time, the trip is easier on my stomach, and I don't feel dizzy as Lorenzo tugs on my hand, leading me out of the Speculis. Laughter, giggles and music echo down the corridor from the distance, and there is a faint sweet smell in the warm air.

Lorenzo glances down the corridor, a playful smile lighting up his face, before he nods in the other direction from the fun he clearly wants to join. Nothing looks familiar, but the corridors all look the same somehow as we head down a few corridors and through two doors until we come to an arched pair of doors with long oak handles that spread across the entire door. It's not guarded, and no sound comes from inside the room as Lorenzo casually strolls up to the doors and pulls them both open. The doors creak, adding a much-needed sound as Lorenzo nods his head for me to go inside.

Lorenzo's voice is nothing more than a whisper as I pass him. "Flash him a pretty smile, and he won't be such a dick."

I barely hold in the chuckle in my throat, but my mouth feels dry as my footsteps echo on the dark tiles, the surface so clean I can see my reflection. It's quite clear this is a personal space, and everything is designed for comfort, echoed by the rich and vibrant colors. Several comfy chairs face a lit fireplace, and in the corners lie tall bookcases, a rich coffee-stained table, and thick dark red rugs. Thick garnet curtains are held back from the long, tall windows by dark rope ties, and a fae light brushes against my cheek as it passes me, leaving an icy sting. At the far end of the room are four pillars cut into the shape of a familiar female, her hands outstretched like she is holding the ceiling up with her palms alone.

The goddess.

These pillar statues are just like the one in Junepit City, but much smaller. The goddess statue in Junepit City, which I've seen in paintings, is taller than the entire city and right dead in the center, water pouring out of the tip of her sword and into the sea. I've always wanted to see it for myself. One day, I will.

The pillars give way to a balcony outside, and in the middle of them is Emerson. The sinfully dark king. The monster the world fears. His wings are stretched out, the wind softly blowing against them, and they look as dark as the black mountains in front of him. His muscular form is something to behold, and I run my eyes over every inch of him, drinking in the view. He is magnificent.

I take a few more steps until I'm by one of the chairs near the fire, and Emerson tilts his head to the side, his midnight purple eyes locking onto mine, and a flicker of fear bounces in my chest from the raw anger I find. His skin is such a dark grey, his horns shine like onyx in the night, where they belong. I can feel his power like an old song, stretching and pushing the limits of this room and wrapping around me. His power can be felt everywhere, I bet even at the end of this world.

I stand still, like a doe in front of a bright light, like he always nicknames me as. "You asked to see me?"

The dark pits of swirling purple in his eyes seem to make their own storm as he turns and, in four long strides, he is right in front of me. His voice is a mixture of a growl and anger. "Where were you tonight?"

Tilting my head to the side, I note the fury and something else flashing across his face. "You damn well know. I was at work."

He growls deep and low, sending shivers down my spine. "With the mortal male?"

"Yes," I snap before sighing, feeling tired and restless, my skin itching to argue with him until both of us can't think straight. "Truthfully, I have had a shitty night, and I'm not interested in your bad mood. Go and find another mortal who might be interested. Or fae. Or whatever."

I walk around him, well aware the dangerous monster is watching me like prey, and I slump into a chair, which is far too comfy even with its strange back made for wings. I expect Emerson to storm out, to leave me here to wallow, but instead he sits down in the chair near me, and I find my eyes fixated on how he spreads his legs out, his thighs thick with toned muscle. The Wyerns must work out every day to look like that. His hands dig into the armrests as he looks over at me from head to toe before grunting to himself.

"Most mortals run in fear when I'm angry. Why don't you?"

"I feel like that was a rhetorical question, but I'm going to answer. You're scary, but I've faced worse, and they have always wanted to kill me. I figure you might be mad, but you need me alive. Which makes you the less frightening monster for now."

He stays looking at the fire, but I can see the color of the flames washing over his face. The flames make the purple of his eyes light up, reminding me of sunset bluebells that grew outside one of the schools I went to. I'd pick dozens of them and wrap them in ribbon as a gift for my foster mom. I almost smile at the memory, how normal it was, how safe and happy I was for a time.

"You were on a date with Merrick Night."

His voice is flat, but there is a note of anger still there... of what I might suspect is jealousy if I didn't know better.

I climb off the seat and walk closer to the fire. "It wasn't a date. It was work."

Emerson's laugh is hollow. "He wants to fuck you, in all the ways I've thought of fucking you. I've thought of more. Up the wall, in that tiny bed of yours, in my bed or over my desk. Do you know where I thought of fucking you the most?"

Heat prickles over my skin, and everything tightens. He's a monster. A monster, Calliophe. Get it together.

All my own warnings fade into nothing, and I block out the rational voice in my head as he finishes. "I've thought of pulling you on my lap, on my goddess-damned throne, and fucking you in front of my entire court. So they know you're mine."

Mine.

Mine.

Mine.

Words feel foreign as I reply, as I lie. "Well, keep those thoughts to yourself, because I'm working for you, and you're the king of an enemy race, and that can never happen. I don't know when we crossed a boundary, but we have."

His words are cruel. "You mean I broke down those walls you have up to protect yourself from getting hurt?"

Anger ripples across my body as I swing around and storm up to him. He looks up at me from his seat, a smirk on his lips. "You know what? What does anything about me have to do with you? I'm allowed to date who I like. I'm allowed to do what I like and who I like. You're someone I just met and work for. When this is all over, we will never see each other again."

He stands up swiftly, leaving no space between our touching bodies, and his rough hand grabs my throat, his sharp nails pressing in. On instinct, I pull my dagger out and place the blade against his throat, pressing hard enough to draw his attention to it, but not enough to cut him. The amusement in his eyes matches the almost catlike smile that blooms on his face as he looks down at me. "Do it. It will take a lot more than slitting my throat to kill me, mortal."

"You think I wouldn't? Let me go!"

He growls, taunting me. "If you want me to not think of fucking you, doing this isn't working. It does the opposite."

I can feel something hard pressing into my stomach, and it takes everything in me not to pay attention to it. He is the king. A monster used to getting everything and everyone he wants. I won't be another toy for the monster.

I growl back at the monster in front of me, and his lips tilt further up, revealing his sharp canines. Sometimes it's so easy to forget he's a monster. He's so beautiful in his own way. Supernatural, immortal and old magic simply exists around him. I can taste it in the air, over his alluring scent. I'm not sure which is more dangerous to want more of.

All of this is a game to him. We both know it. My dagger might be pressed against his throat, but his hand is wrapped around my neck. I know that he could snap my neck and take my life in a second, and I wouldn't stand a chance to even cut him. A monster playing with his mortal toy. He leans closer, and I keep my dagger steady for whatever he is going to do. He leans his head into my neck, strands of my hair brushing over his cheek, and he takes a deep breath.

Scenting me.

He groans deeply, and the sound sets all of my body alight. "Don't go on a date with him again. He is dangerous."

"Merrick?"

Emerson's teeth graze at my neck, and I go still. "Don't say another male's name while you're with me. Especially not one you've been on a date with."

"It wasn't a date," I argue, even when it feels fruitless. "And stop commanding me. You're not my king."

His lips, rough and strong, press against my neck, and my legs feel weak. All of me feels weak. I try to push down the soft urge to try and fix the handsome monster in front of me, convincing me that I'd stand a chance of actually fixing his corrupt, dark, and broken soul. My breath hitches, and I feel like my heart is climbing up my throat just as the door opens, and I lurch away from him. He lets me go, and I lower my dagger, looking over to see Zurine in the doorway, clearly astonished.

Zurine looks like she's caught in headlights

as she pauses, looking between us before calling her face into a more neutral expression. "Calliophe, I heard that you had arrived. I imagined you might be tired after a long day, and your room is all set up. I designed everything for you."

Emerson laughs low, going back to his seat. "Careful, Zur, if you spoil the mortal, she might never stop being your best and only friend."

I'm sure there is an underlying joke I don't get as Zurine glares at her king before looking back at me, giving me a tense smile. "Would you like me to walk you to your room?"

"I'd love that," I say, carefully sliding my dagger back and refusing to look once at Emerson, who I know is still looking at me from the feel of his eyes like another presence in the room. Like a dark shadow.

Zurine is still looking at Emerson, and I can't read her expression other than a hint of sadness there. She gently touches my arm. "Give me two seconds."

I nod. "I'll wait outside."

Zurine shuts the door, and I stand in the empty corridor for a second, wondering if they know that I have strong hearing that most mortals don't. Nothing they say will be a secret while I'm so close.

"It's not her." Zurine's muffled voice is full of anguish.

"Get out, Zur, I'm not in the mood. Lorenzo has already said it. So have Felix and Nathiel."

She huffs. "Then listen to us. We are your court, promised in blood to protect and serve you. Protecting you means stopping you from destroying yourself on an impossible hope."

Emerson doesn't reply.

"Calliophe is a brave mortal, fierce and loyal. I understand why you might think... but she's gone."

A growl vibrates the very walls, and I flinch. "How do you know for certain? How can any of us ever know? Prophecies, all of it, was just bullshit to take her from me."

"Every time, she was my best friend, and I would know. You loved her so deeply not even the stars or gods could part you. You'd know too."

The silence stretches on. He has an ex, I'm guessing, someone he loved deeply, and I hate the jealousy I feel. "I miss her too."

"Get out," Emerson asks, but this time he

sounds defeated, and something in my chest cracks at that voice.

I step back when I hear Zurine's heels clicking on the tiles, right before she opens the door and flashes me a smile. I'm not sure if it's fake, not after hearing all that, but I'm sure that as a fae, she has mastered how to control pretty smiles and fake emotions. Who does Emerson think I am? What prophecy? Who was this person they both clearly loved?

I know I won't get the answers, and I'm not going to ask, as I don't want to be any more involved with this court than I already am.

I need to finish this job and leave. That's what is best for us all.

We walk in silence down the corridor and take a left, past a metal-framed painting of the black mountains themselves, the stars littering the sky in many constellations. My eyes wash over the painting, admiring how beautiful it is. It's not a masterpiece or perfectly done, but it has its own uniqueness that catches my eye.

Zurine looks between the painting and me as we walk away from it. "That was painted on Nocturno, a thousand years ago by the previous queen. I never got to meet her."

No wonder I like it. It was painted on my birthday.

"When did she die?" I quietly ask. In the book I've read, they talk about a king and queen of the Wyerns who never had an heir. Clearly, they did have an heir, but the history book doesn't know about him, or it doesn't talk about him other than mentions of a new ruler. The lights down here are warmer, and the wind whistles through the stone on this side of the castle, comforting me even in this strange place.

Zurine's voice is soft. "Many years ago. Emerson was only young himself. It's a tragedy our court and people do not speak often of, but we do like to remind ourselves with her paintings."

I get that. If the Fae Queen died, the fae would mourn for years. Decades. "I hope I didn't put my foot in."

"No," she quickly replies. "No. You are welcome to ask some questions. It's only natural, and it isn't a secret. Many know of her death in Ethereal City."

Our conversation drifts off as we finally come to a row of five doors at the end of a corridor, with a table with flowers by the wall.

I take in the beautiful fae female in front of me. "In the history book I read on your court's race, Wyerns have always been monsters. Both in looks and in actions. But not a word tells the truth about them. They aren't just those things."

"The world may call anyone a monster when the villain is writing the story."

I'm silent, lost for words as Zurine presses her hand upon the oak door, and it shimmers, gold dust flickering across the flat surface before a gold knob appears in the center. "If I were you, I'd stay in your room. Not all members of my court are agreeable to mortals, and there are guests visiting tonight for celebrations. They respect Emerson's demand to stay away from you, but I wouldn't push it."

"Why would they bother hurting me when I'm helping them?"

"Cocks and egos are a terrible mix for males. They should try thinking like us females at least sometimes," she smoothly suggests. "Sleep well, my friend."

"Friends don't keep secrets," I whisper, knowing she can hear me as she walks away.

She flicks her hair over her shoulder. "Immortal friends do. Good night."

I head inside the room and shut the door, only to pause. I don't know what I was expecting of the room, but it wasn't this. By the goddess, this might be the best sleep I've ever had. I'm amazed as I step further into the bedroom in front of me. It's utterly stunning. The whole room has white stone pillars, swirls in the stone, and a detailed ceiling of similar markings. Fae lights hover around the ceiling, moving softly into places, but it isn't too bright, it's a perfect lighting. The bed is right in the center of the room, a massive circular-shaped bed with black satin sheets and white throw cushions on top of many, many pillows. There's a massive balcony attached to the room, nearly taking up the entire left wall, and there is a wall of glass to stop the breeze coming in, with glass doors in the center. I walk across to it, enjoying the lush cream carpets and running my fingers over the mirror-covered chest of drawers. I open the sliding glass doors, the cold breeze blowing over me and making me shiver as I look out, the black mountains as endless as the stars.

Someone shoots past my balcony, like a falling star blasting through the night, wings sparkling like black onyx. I barely recognize Emerson for a moment as he spreads his wings out and simply lets the wind glide him through the air.

I watch him go into the far distance until he is nothing more than a speck, and only then do I realize that my heart has never beat as fast as it does when I'm around him. Even when he is flying away.

CHAPTER
FIFTEEN

My dreams appear like glittering stars, shaped into windows of my life, and I am helpless but to watch as they pass me, one after another. A brief flash of each memory, each haunting, cold and empty chunk of my past until it gets to the worst memory. This star bursts into my view, throwing me back into the past. Louie is so young as he grabs my hand, pulling me to the door, trying to protect me like he has been told all brothers do. But no one can protect me from my monster.

Louie cries out in terror as my monster takes up the end of the corridor, and I see nothing but its massive bat wings. My foster mom jumps out from the bedroom, between us, and looks right back at me.

"RUN!"

She turns back to my monster as he lifts his clawed hand, sharp black nails stretching out to us and warm magic spreading across the room. My foster dad runs out of the bedroom next, whatever magic my monster used to keep them back gone, and he looks right at me before jumping in front of the nasty bolt of magic aimed right at us. The bitter magic goes straight for his chest, and his body slams into my foster mom, both of them going through the wall. I don't know when I start screaming, but I don't stop. Rage, anger and pain only increase my scream until all I see is bright pink light before I pass out.

I wake up with my heart racing, my bedsheets stuck to me and damp. I crawl off the bed as quickly as I can, bounding for the balcony and opening the glass doors with a slam. I suck in a great heap of harsh cold air, letting the cold remind me that I'm here. Not in the past. I'm not a child anymore, unable to defend myself. Eventually my breathing evens out, and I place my hand on my neck for a few minutes, watching the glittering black mountains. It must be late. I doubt I slept that long. I glance back at the bed, cringing at the damp sheets. I'm not sleeping anytime soon.

When I'm no longer shaking and as calm as I'm going to get, I head back inside and go through my drawers, realizing I definitely should have packed an overnight bag. There are several pieces of clothing in here, a corset with a long skirt attached to the bottom, or tight leather pants with a styled sleeveless leather vest made of the same leather that the Wyerns wear. I go to the bottom drawer and find leggings and a men's blue shirt. That will do. I pull them on, the shirt falling to my knees. I use the bathroom and freshen up before looking at the bed one more time and deciding to ignore Zurine's warnings not to leave my room.

I can handle myself around monsters. The corridors are silent as I step out in my boots, looking around and wondering who is in the other rooms. I follow the way we came, back to the cozy room Emerson was in, which is now empty, and down past a larger room that comes out to another corridor with ledges on the left side, likely for the Wyerns to easily jump out.

I'm about to give up and go back to my room instead of getting lost when I hear the beautiful sound of a piano being played nearby. The song is old, a deep and haunting melody played by fast and quick fingers. Whoever's playing is extremely skilled, and the urge to find out makes me follow the sound until I find the right door. The door is cracked open a little, light pouring out into the corridor from inside. I softly push the door further open enough to peek through.

A Wyern male that I don't know sits at the piano completely mesmerized as he plays it, his fingers fast moving across the keys. His hair is a dark grey, his wings are littered with dark grey scars and hang low on his back, on the floor. He's wearing nothing but a grey robe, and despite the fact he looks around my age, the way he holds himself, the greyness of his hair, and his thin skin tell me he is much, much older. I wonder how old supernaturals have to be before they turn grey. For mortals, it's about fifty years. I know the Fae Queen has only just started going grey, according to rumors, and she's thousands of years old. I step into the room, and he pauses, the beautiful song ending.

He looks over at me, his eyes sharper than any supernatural I've met. Old. He is very, very old. I feel like he sees right through me, and in the moments of silence, he picks apart my soul to find what he is looking for. I feel like I'm in danger, and goose bumps spread across my body. "I should go. I'm sorry for interrupting you."

The male blinks and shakes his head. On his hand are three rings: gold, emerald green and silver. They flash as he makes a high-pitched noise on the keyboard. "Stay."

"I'm Calliophe," I say, walking over to him. If he wanted to hurt me, there's a good chance he would have done so by now.

His eyes soften just a little. "Cornelius."

"All the best people have names starting with a *C*," I say, stopping at his side. He waves his hand at the space on the bench, and I sit down.

"Do you play, Calliophe?"

I clear my throat, touching a key and the sound ringing around the room. "No."

He smiles at me, his canines much longer than Emerson's, touching his bottom lip. "How unfortunate. I will teach you. Every night at the midnight hour in this room."

I don't say yes or agree to anything, but Cornelius begins showing me how to play, and I bet he has taught someone before, as it seems easy to him. At least an hour passes by until I'm smiling and laughing with Cornelius as I finally manage a simple lullaby.

Cornelius takes over, playing a new song that is upbeat and makes me want to dance. "So, who are you in this court? I was told only family and close friends live here."

"I am this court," he answers simply, not telling me anything somehow too.

"Oh, right. Can I ask how old you are? Never seen a supernatural with grey hair."

He laughs. "Every time, you always ask exactly the wrong questions or the right ones to some people."

"What do you mean, 'every time'?"

He looks right at me, his eyes like green pits of frozen moss. "I should have stopped it. The curse."

"Curse? What curse?"

"Right question, for once," he smoothly replies and places his hand on my shoulder. "Never stop asking questions, Calliophe."

The door cracks open again, and almost like a fae light blinking off, Cornelius's smile fades away, and he lowers his hand from my shoulder. He goes back to the piano and starts playing a sad song this time, ignoring that I'm there altogether. I look over to see Lorenzo in the doorway, light highlighting the confused expression on his face.

He waves a hand for me to come over, and I turn back to my new friend. "Thank you, Cornelius. Midnight hour, I'll try to remember."

He doesn't answer me or even acknowledge my presence, and I'm frowning as I walk away and out into the corridor to Lorenzo. Lorenzo pulls the door shut behind me and crosses his arms before he laughs.

A deep, throaty laugh. "Did he talk to you?"

"Who, Cornelius?" I ask, and Lorenzo nods. "Yes, he invited me in and taught me to play a song. I think he was too nice to tell me I suck at learning any musical instruments."

Lorenzo laughs harder at that, and he

stinks of booze and sex, but he can't be that drunk. "What is wrong with you? Who is he?"

He stumbles to me, the smell worse up close. He puts his hands on my shoulders. "That's my father. King Cornelius Eveningstar."

His laugh is the only thing keeping my legs from feeling weak. The king who started a war that killed millions. He is older than the Fae Queen, from what I've read. "The male who just taught you how to play the piano hasn't spoken to anyone in the court for a hundred years. He hasn't left here either."

"What?" I whisper.

"He lost his mind, damn witches and their curses. Our race is—" He pauses like he remembers he is speaking to me. That mention of a curse again. "I've not heard a word from him, and I'm not sure if I'm so fucking drunk right now that I'm imagining all this."

"It's real," I mutter. "What curse? Cornelius mentioned a curse, too."

He throws his arm around my shoulder, pulling me to his side. "Seems like everyone in my family likes you."

I shake my head as he throws me off the

question of curses. "You need to sleep the booze off."

"Is that an invitation to your bed?"

I whack his rock-hard chest, and he bellows with laughter. "No."

"Shame," he sighs and looks at me for a long moment. "I have no interest in hurting you, just so you know that. I'm your friend."

"We barely know each other."

He holds his hand to his chest. "Every time I'm in your presence, you stab me with your words. Be kind."

"You're so dramatic," I say, but I'm smiling and can't stop.

Lorenzo stops us outside my room, and I'm surprised we got here so quickly. "Get back in your room, mortal, before Zurine finds you out here and gets mad."

"I'm not in danger here...," I say.

The pretty playboy expression fades away, and for a moment, I see the warrior beneath it. A member of Emerson's court. A Wyern Prince. "You just found yourself alone in a room with a thousand-year-old Wyern King who has lost his mind and his good senses. That king went to war and murdered thousands, if not hundreds of thousands of your race, and enjoyed it. He drank mortal blood and ripped them to pieces for sport. You tell me if you aren't in any danger."

I gulp, getting the point as I try not to be frightened in front of him. He surprises me by tugging me in for a hug, and he squeezes me tightly for a moment before letting go. "Don't leave your room until morning. Zurine will come for you."

He waits for me to go inside and shut the door behind me, and I lean my head against it. Lorenzo is right. I'm not safe here, and I need to be careful.

I walk back to the bed, pausing when I scent Emerson. He was here. I look around for him, finding the room empty, until I notice my bedsheets have been changed, and there is a yellow bound book on my pillow. I pick the book up, chuckling as I read the title. It's the second book in the series that I was reading. Sitting on my bed, I open the first page and smile to myself.

Everyone needs a monster who brings them romance books.

HEIR OF MONSTERS

A BANG WAKES ME UP, and I jolt upright, a ripple of magic in the very air around my bed. I blink, rubbing my eyes and wondering what the hell that was when my door slams open and a monster fills the doorframe.

It's not Emerson.

Or any Wyern I know. Three Wyern males flood into my room, one after the other, and for a second, I'm frozen in pure fear. I search around my bed, remembering I'm only wearing a large shirt, and find only the romance book to use as a weapon. I hold it and glance at the dresser, where my daggers are, and back to the males. All of them are unfamiliar, but each of them has dark black hair and looks similar enough to conclude they're clearly brothers. They're not as muscular as most of the Wyerns I've seen, but they are big enough. I know I'd struggle to take them all down on my own. I'd be better jumping off the flipping balcony.

I leap for the dresser and only get to the end of my bed before a wave of magic slams into my chest and throws me backwards. The air is smacked from my lungs, and my head slams against the headboard with a crunch. I cry out in pain as I fall on the pillows, tasting blood in my mouth. I lean up, glowering at them as all three of them crawl around my bed until I'm surrounded. Another whip of magic slams the bedroom door shut, locking us in, and the icy sting stays around the room. This is bad. This is really bad.

My voice is more of a screech. "You're not allowed in here. Get the fuck out!" I scream. "Emerson! Zurine! Lorenzo! HELP!"

The male in the middle, at the end of the bed, cruelly laughs. "Pathetic mortal. My magic won't let a sound out of here. Scream all you like."

"At least she has nice legs. Doesn't smell like he is fucking her, though."

The other one bellows in laughter, his eyes eating me up. "We should see if her pussy is as nice as the rest of her. Part fae, but I bet she still feels as fucking good as any fae cunt."

My cheeks redden, and a new fear becomes apparent. Fuck no. They aren't having me. I'd rather die.

The one on the left lunges for me, and I lift

the book, smacking him across the face with it. He actually pauses, and blood pours from his cheek. Paper cut. Book cut. Whatever it is, I know I made it worse for myself, but that was damn satisfying. He bares his teeth at me, leaning closer. "I was going to be quick and lessen your suffering. But now…"

"I'm sure being quick is normal for you. Sorry, I'm just not interested in a one-minute lame experience with your small dick," I snap before kicking him in the chest. He grabs my leg with a grunt and holds me in place, tightening his grip on my ankle.

His brother leans down, diving his face in my neck and breathing me in. "Do you know what we do to mortals like you for fun?"

"Three against one. Real big masculine power show going on here. Further proof of how small your dick is," I mutter, refusing to show fear. Refusing to give them exactly what they want even if I am winding them up at this point.

"The king's pretty pink bitch sure has a mouth on her."

"I can think of a way of shutting her up," the male who isn't touching me states.

"He'll kill you if you touch me. He'll know it's you," I bite out, but my heart is racing so hard, so loud, I can't think straight through the sheer terror in my chest.

"No, he won't. We will be gone before he even finds what is left of you," the one I slapped states. He lashes out, grabbing my arm and pulling it up to his mouth. I scream out in pain as his sharp canine teeth dig straight into my skin. There's a deep, gnawing, sucking sensation as he holds onto my arm and drinks from me. I kick and smack at him, only for one of the others to grab my other arm and hold me tight as he bites straight into me. I kick, scream, fight with everything I have until I suddenly begin to feel weak, for my body to go slack in their hold. Their hands roll across my body, touching me everywhere, and yet I feel nothing.

My eyes find the male at the end of the bed, watching his brothers feed on me, desire burning in his dark eyes. He undoes his belt, the sound horrid. "No one's going to save you now, but don't worry, I won't be quick and disappoint."

They're going to kill me. They're going to

rape me first and then kill me. Tears fill my eyes as everything gets groggy, and I vaguely see the male taking his shirt off, throwing it on the bed. *Emerson. I need you. Someone come and save me. Please, please don't let me die here.* I haven't cried in front of anyone in years, and I never wanted to, but nothing will stop the tears flooding down my cheeks. Suddenly, there's an icy chill that goes through the room right before a smack of a door, and a blast gushes around me like a heavy breeze. I collapse on the bed, black star-like dust falling around my arms where the males were... and now they are just gone.

Oh my goddess, they are the dust. I feel breathless as I watch the male at the end of the bed collapse to his knees, bowing his head low and whimpering as he shakes. "It was just so fun, my king. We weren't going to kill her... but-t my brothers. You killed my brothers over a mortal bitch!"

"Mine!"

I turn my head to see Emerson standing in the doorframe, filling it as his terrifying voice fills the room, and my heart feels like it could explode in my chest from relief. If I thought

Emerson was scary before when we were arguing, it is nothing on the cold expression he is wearing now.

He is livid.

I shiver as his eyes stay on the male, locking onto him with an unnatural predator gaze, and he is across the room in seconds. "Plea—"

Emerson lifts the male up by his neck, holding him like he weighs nothing. "Please d-don't."

"There is no mercy for males like you in my court."

Before I can even blink, Emerson slams his hand into the male's chest, and with his black, sharp nails, he rips out his heart as the male roars. He holds the beating heart in front of him as the male slowly dies, screaming and crying for his brothers. His screams and roars shake the very ground underneath us with his power, but it's nothing on Emerson. He barely notices the power of the dying Wyern. Like a fly bugging a nest of wasps.

The silent, cold, unflinching male in front of me is the king of Wyerns. Now more than ever, and it takes my breath away.

He drags what is left of the male to the balcony and opens the doors before easily throwing him off the edge of the balcony, his heart next.

Silence ticks on, each second longer than the next, before Emerson finally looks back at me. "Do you want me to leave?"

"No," I breathe out, my cheeks still wet with tears, my bottom lip wobbling.

His eyes flicker with surprise before he storms over to me and gently picks me up, helping me get comfy and sit up against the headboard. He examines my head, my leg, and the wounds on my wrists. His jaw looks ready to snap from the pressure of his frown as his magic takes over, washing over me like a cold but soothing glow.

"I didn't know you actually bite," I murmur when his magic stops and nothing hurts anymore. I still feel tired, so so tired.

"On occasion," he coolly replies.

I search his eyes for what is going on in his head, my voice hoarse. "Thank you for saving me. Twice now."

His growl should frighten me, but it doesn't. "They should have never touched you.

I should have spent the next week torturing them for it."

My heart pounds as I glance at the blood on his hands, the blood sprayed on his clothes. He looks down and wipes the blood on his shirt. "Why didn't you kill the last male in the same way you did the first two? Does that magic only work on a small amount of people?"

His lips twitch for a moment. "Even injured and exhausted, you never stop asking questions."

I purse my lips, waiting for a response. "Well, don't I deserve the answer?"

He might even smile for a moment before frowning again. "No, my power isn't limited. I was born different, and if I wished, I could easily kill a hundred with the click of my fingers and leave only star dust behind."

My insides freeze. I wish I didn't ask. "Star dust?"

"A side effect from using the night to kill," he grunts. "I killed the first two in pure anger. I should have made them suffer. I got control of myself just enough to make the other male suffer more. It wasn't enough."

I lean over and place my hand on his thigh, yawning slightly. His eyes latch onto my hand, and a new but familiar tension builds between us. "It was. Thank you."

"Lie down, Doe," he demands, seeing how tired I am, his lips a thin line. I look at the scales on the side of his face and lift my hand, running my finger down the sharp edges. He stays still the entire time, closing his eyes for a moment. "Still a monster."

I shake my head, lowering my hand. "On the outside, maybe, but I see through it."

He grunts and points at the bed. "Lie down and rest. Now."

"Bossy boots," I yawn. "Only if you read to me."

He smirks. "Did you get to the part where he sits Desandra on the edge of the window and fucks her in front of her husband, who is cutting the grass with his magic?"

I snort in laughter. "No, but it sounds delicious. Read it to me."

He sighs and picks up the book, making himself at home on the bed. I crawl to his side, pulling my pillow under my head, and his magic wraps a blanket around me, one of his wings tucking me in close.

With the heat coming off him, with his deep spoken words lulling me to sleep, I don't fear a thing because I realize that in those last moments, when I knew I was going to die, it was him that I was calling out for. It was his name on my lips. In those last moments, I begged for the monster to save me. And he did.

CHAPTER
SIXTEEN

The weeks soon roll into a month, and my progress is pretty much summed up as I glance at the newspaper in a stall, with a portrait of the Fae Prince on the front page and the title "Still Missing" above it. The Fae Prince is classically beautiful, as most fae are, with his silvery blond hair tucked behind tall spiked fae ears and light purple eyes, cute smile and golden skin. The heir to the throne looks much like the Fae Queen paintings I've seen.

I sigh and walk away from the stall, back to work. A month has passed since the princess and prince went missing, and I'm not a step closer to figuring anything out. I head right into my office, chatting with Wendy for a moment and shutting the door behind me. I bury my mind in the fae symbol book in front of me, looking for the one I've seen from Lorenzo's drawing, and the hours stretch on until I'm near the end of the book, and still nothing. I want to scream in frustration, but I hold the noise back.

The noise from my door handle turning draws my attention, and seconds later Merrick walks in like he owns the place.

I glare at him. Things have been weird since our date/not-date, and I'm not sure how to fix it. Or if I even want to with how complicated things are in my life. "Have you heard of knocking?"

Merrick looks pissy. "Come with me and grab the siren on your way."

He walks out, not giving me a chance to outright refuse, and I grumble about moody ass bosses as I leave my office and go to Nerelyth's office next door. Like a half decent mortal, I knock twice before waiting for her to call me in.

"You don't have to knock, you know?" Nerelyth says in greeting.

I snort. "I think knocking is the only way not to be rude."

She gives me a quizzical look and closes the ancient-looking book she was reading as I look around. Seashells are littered across her desk, and woven seaweed hangs in patterns on the wall behind her desk. In the center of her desk is a Loco Sphere, the only expensive thing I've seen Nerelyth have—and it makes me suspect she once had money. Loco Spheres are rare magic, contained in a glass sphere, and whoever owns it, it becomes the truth of their heart. Inside this sphere is a crashing wave, smashing violently into the green sea.

I've always wondered what it would show of me. Of my heart.

"Merrick wants us," I inform her. "He is in a brilliant mood today, as always."

She groans, standing up. "He needs a good fucking, that one."

I know the next words out of her mouth before she even says them. "I'm sure you could volunteer for that and he would be a much more delightful person to your bestie."

I laugh. "I'm not sleeping with our boss so he leaves you alone."

"Then do it for your vagina," she joyfully replies, and my cheeks burn as I roll my eyes. "We both know she would be thankful."

"Come on," I say, and she laughs, the sound sweeter than candy as she hooks her arm through mine and we head together to the stairs where Merrick isn't waiting as he usually does. We look between each other and find him by the steel doors under the stairs on the other side, a big sign above saying No Entry. None of us are allowed in here, except Merrick and a few special enforcers that work down there, and they are always exactly silent about what shit happens down there, even when Nerelyth and I got them drunk that one time. Nerelyth suspects they have been blood sworn to the queen and commanded by her power not to say a word.

I'm still yawning as we walk over, reminding me about the late night I had with Zurine and the royal court cellar, where we stayed up drinking some very expensive-tasting wines until we couldn't hardly walk back to our rooms. I suspect the impaired walking was more me than Zurine, but she was tipsy. She listened to me talk endlessly about my life, the parts of it I enjoyed, and yet never once asked me to stop talking. It's only now I realize she told me nothing new about her. It was one of the more interesting weekends I've had there. Most of the time, the Wyerns now completely ignore me, like they are scared to even look my way. Except for Lorenzo, of course. I haven't seen Emerson in nearly three weeks, and I hate that I miss the grumpy bastard. I think he's ignored me since the night of the attack because of unnecessary guilt. Or he just got bored with me. It's likely the second one.

Other than dealing with a bored Lorenzo and a shopping-addicted Zurine, who loves to buy me new clothes—enough to fill that castle—I spend my midnight hours with Cornelius. Every night that I'm there, I sneak out and play the piano with him. I know I shouldn't spend time with him, but I've always had a weakness for someone who clearly needs help. I don't know why he reached out to me, but something tells me I should turn up every single time. I also know I'm never really alone. Lorenzo doesn't bother to hide his footsteps outside the door. I find it hard to believe

Cornelius was ever the king that I've read about, the murderous evil king that everyone should fear. To me, he's just this funny, charming old male who teaches me piano with patience and kindness, like he is teaching a child. It might be foolish and a bit dangerous to go spend time alone with him, but if he is solely talking to me, an hour of my time isn't much to give.

Other than that, it's boring in that castle, cold, and most doors are firmly locked with magic, so I don't even get to explore. To make things worse, I don't even have a romance book to read, and Emerson hasn't returned the one he stole yet.

I know he's just keeping it to be petty at this point. But no matter how many times I walk around the castle, seeing Lorenzo on occasion, I don't find Emerson. I push away thoughts of the Wyern King as Merrick types in the long password code in the magical lock for the door before cutting his finger and dripping the blood against the magic seal before the door slides open. We all head inside, and the steel door shuts right behind us with a harsh slam. Dim fae light leads down a long passageway, which opens into a domed room.

The room is completely made of steel walls that wrap all the way around it, and in the center are cages. Dozens, likely hundreds, of cages. The cages are stacked above each other, going all the way up to the ceiling in rows and rows. There must be hundreds of monsters in here, if not a thousand, and it is silent. How is it so silent? I look over at the steel doors to my left, knowing this building goes really far back, and I wonder how many rooms full of monsters there are.

"You want to see the hybrid?" Merrick asks, and I nod. I asked weeks ago, but he shooed me out of his office without giving me a reply. "Well, I finally got your permission. One-time visit, and you have five minutes."

"This has been here the whole time?" I ask.

He looks over his shoulder as he walks away from us. "Where else is safe, Miss Sprite?"

"I love when he calls you Miss Sprite. It's so sexy," Nerelyth whispers to me.

My voice is sarcastic. "Yes, Miss Mist."

She giggles, and I shake my head as we

follow after Merrick. There are rope-pulled platforms in each row, several of them, leading up to different levels to view and feed the monsters, I'm guessing. The silence is daunting, and I look into the cages, which are blacked out from what looks like black smoke inside, and wonder what is hiding in them. I pause when we walk past a cage with a tiny, small starfish in the middle.

Nerelyth shivers and clutches my arm. "I'm never going to nap at work again with that thing in here."

"What is it? It's cute," I ask, admiring the pink starfish with bright, crystal blue eyes and glittering scales.

She looks at me with wide eyes. "A demoneater. You don't even want to know what that will do to you. There are pits deep in the sea where they breed, and no one ever comes back from there."

I glance at the cute pink starfish one more time, and I swear a voice purrs in my ear. "Come closer, mortal of strange, old blood."

Shivering, I cling to Nerelyth and hurry up after Merrick. I get the urge to look in every one of the cages, to see all the many monsters they've caught over the years, to understand why each one of them turned into a monster in the first place. Were they born a monster? Turned? Cursed?

But I don't look, knowing better. This is a dome of nightmares. We come to the last row, and Merrick holds open the door of the metal rope-pulled lift for us to step in. It's a tight fit, and Merrick's whole body is pressed to my side when he climbs on and pulls the rope. The weight slowly drops on the other side, pulling us up, and I try to ignore Merrick's body pressed against mine. The lift stops when Merrick wishes it, and it must be enchanted. He opens the door, offering a hand to help me out. I take it, his palm warm in mine, and wait for Nerelyth. She pales when she looks down.

"I hate heights."

I rest my head on her shoulder for a moment as Merrick stops in front of a cage blacked out with smoke like the others, magic of some kind. Merrick presses his palm onto the metal bar, and the smoke slowly fades away until the hybrid appears, curled up in a ball on the floor. It looks up, dead at me, and screeches.

Oh, it remembers me alright. Its body is bent, bones coming out of its back, and I go around the cage to get a better look. When I'm close to the bars, his back emits a pink glow. When he howls to the skies, I see the symbol on his back, and that's where the pink light is coming from. It's the same one Lorenzo drew in his notes, so this hybrid was made by the same person, and this symbol must be a clue.

"Does it always do that? I ask, looking at Merrick.

"I wouldn't know," he replies, looking lost in his own thoughts. The fae symbol, the same that Lorenzo marked, is quite large, and it's clearly been drawn by something sharp into the hybrid's skin.

"It's creepy. Urgh," Nerelyth says to no one in particular.

"Imagine an army of them," I mutter.

"I'd rather not, Miss Sprite. Are you done?" Merrick snips.

"Yes," I sharply reply. "That's all I need to see."

"Good, we can leave," Nerelyth says, hightailing it back to the platform lift.

Merrick catches my arm before I can follow

her, his voice low. "Keep your mouth shut about the pink glow. Got it?"

I pull my arm from him. "Whatever."

We all head into the lift, and I make sure he presses against Nerelyth on the way down, and I try my best to ignore him.

"We should kill them. Keeping them in here to be observed is cruel. Most of these monsters were once real people," Nerelyth muses out loud.

I nod at her. "I agree, but I wouldn't like to be the one to kill the cute starfish."

Nerelyth hisses. "That is not a starfish, Calli."

When we come out of the steel door and back into the reception area, Merrick storms off without another word. "Have a good rest of the day, boss!"

I raise an eyebrow at Nerelyth. "Suck up."

She chuckles. "You do not want to know the dirty comeback that came to my head right then."

Laughing, I walk with her back to the offices. "I don't need to. My mind isn't much better."

"That's why you're my bestie," she replies,

bumping my shoulder. "I'm going to do some more work in my office, but I'll have to come over soon. I miss you and Louie. You're working too much."

"Until we find them, I don't see that changing," I whisper back.

"Soon," she vows before walking into her office and closing the door. I head into my office, closing the door behind me.

I nearly jump out of my skin and a weak scream almost escapes my throat when I find Lorenzo leaning on my desk, half sitting on it and eating my tuna fish sandwich I saved for my lunch. With a mouth full, he still looks charming as he grins.

The wall next to him glimmers with mirror magic. After he finishes my lunch, he waves at the wall. "Emerson wants to see you."

"How about no?" I say flatly, turning to lock my door. "I'm at work. It's so dangerous for you to be here."

He grins. "Worried about my pretty face, mortal?"

I shake my head in frustration. "Truthfully, I'm pissed you ate my lunch."

He laughs. "I'll find you some food, don't

worry. You're missing me so badly it's made you grumpy. I get it. Many females have made the same complaint."

"I literally had you sleeping in my apartment for the entire last week," I point out. "It's hard to miss you when you never leave and snore all night. Even that isn't worse than listening to your love story beginning with Posy."

He laughs. "She's not all bad, you know, and I bet in that black heart of hers, she loves the shit out of you."

"I doubt it."

He smiles. "Then you must have a bit of a weakness for monsters."

"She isn't a monster," I mutter.

"I'm sure you called her one when she turned the tap on when you were in the shower last week," he smugly replies.

I glare at him. "Whatever, let's just get this over with."

He looks too happy when I take his hand and he pulls me through the mirror, into the room of mirrors on the other side in the castle. I've sort of gotten used to the layout of the castle now, almost, but even then, I feel lost as

Lorenzo takes me down a flight of stairs to a new level of the castle I haven't been in before. We go through a set of doors that lead to a massive cave room. The walls look like they're made from ancient lava pits, black and earthy, and the scent matches. It's so hot in here, and I think the heat is coming from the ground below.

Right in the center of the room, in a ring of nothing but black wings and male bare chests, is Emerson. He's sparring, I think, with another male while the others cheer and yell. They're in the air, using their wings to almost hover and glide as they slam their swords against each other. My mouth nearly drops open at all the muscle and the damn impressive moves. Emerson counters a hit with his magic, which I'm sure he is barely using, and sends the other male flying back in the air. I blink a few times before I realize it's Felix, one of the Wyerns that I met in the court meeting. Felix has a playful grin on his face as he flips in the air, controlling the hit with his powerful wings and using his own magic to lash through the air with a sort of crackle that almost sounds like embers in a fire. Emerson easily blocks the attack, but Felix is there, flying straight at him and slamming his sword into the gap he left open. Emerson grabs him by the neck and flips him over his shoulder before Felix crashes down to the floor. The males cheer for Emerson as he lands in the middle of the circle, and I look at Lorenzo with a million questions.

Lorenzo leans down. "Sparring, but I'm sure Emerson doesn't always flex his muscles quite that much. Show off."

"So, do you guys spend all your time in here? And can I bring a guest, a bowl of popcorn and a cool drink? This would be much better than sitting at home," I innocently ask. Nerelyth would absolutely love this. I mean, I *love* this.

Lorenzo's barking laugh echoes around, and he wraps his arm around my shoulder. "I can give you a personal show in the bedroom if you like."

I push him away. "Flirting won't get you in my bed."

"What will?" he asks curiously, but it's half-hearted, and I know he doesn't mean it.

We both go silent when Emerson breaks

through the crowd and storms over to me. I run my eyes over his chest this close up, the strange markings on his arm that flicker down to his right pec and the sinful ripples of muscle that make a V-shape into his pants. Holy goddess.

He stops right in front of me, and his expression is sheer ice. "Have you found my sister yet?"

What crawled up his ass and made itself at home?

"No," I answer flatly. "But we might have something. I need more time."

"You best hope my sister has the time you need," he growls.

We've all got an audience, and there are a few whispers. I want to call him out on being an asshole, but with everyone watching, it's not the best time. "Hurry up or you're fired."

"Good luck finding anyone who knows Ethereal City better than an enforcer."

His back is tense as he walks away from me and dismisses me completely, picking a random Wyern to spar with.

Lorenzo shakes his head with a sigh. "Let's

get you some food before you snap and kill my brother for being a moody asshole."

"At least I'm not the only one that thinks he needs to chill."

Lorenzo waits until we are down another set of stairs. His hand is firm on my lower back as he leads me through the castle. "After the attack and kidnap of Solandis, some of our leaders were angry. Solandis being missing is an excuse many have waited for. Emerson has had a lot to deal with, stopping a war. That wasn't about you. Not really."

I don't say anything because it's between Emerson and me, and I think it's about far more than Lorenzo is willing to tell me. We go down two more flights of stairs and through a door into a kitchen space full of counters, hot steam pots, and various other cooking instruments. I haven't seen this place before, and I'm surprised at how cozy it is for a big castle. "This is the family kitchen. Emerson, Solandis and I use it."

"Do you miss her?" I softly ask.

He nods. "We argued, and sometimes I hated her, but mostly I didn't. Maybe she was right about some things and we were both too hotheaded to figure out we aren't on different sides."

I smile as he gets to work, taking out bread and various boxes from the ice storage. He likes cooking, I think. "Being hotheaded does seem to run in the family. Do you want some help with lunch?"

He chuckles. "You remember I've seen what you had in your kitchen. So, no thank you. Have you heard of herbs?"

I frown. "I keep most of that stuff, the ones we could afford, with Louie."

"Ah, the kid brother who eats the leftovers. You should let me cook something fresh for him one day," he muses.

"I think you'd be a terrible influence on him," I admit with a smile. I'm not sure what Louie would make of the Wyerns in general. Let alone Lorenzo.

He laughs. "I'd be on my best behavior."

"I'm not sure even *that* would be enough," I tease.

Lorenzo moves around the kitchen easily, knowing exactly where everything is before he serves me a plate full of several types of bread, cheeses, cooked fish, and various fruits. I dig in as he sits next to me, his shoulder bumping into mine. "Thank you. I was curious, why aren't there any paintings or portraits around the castle of you and Emerson, or your sister?"

He tenses for a second, pausing with a fruit slice in his hand. "There was. Once."

I get the impression that the subject is off limits, and I gulp. "Can I ask you something else?"

Lorenzo finally finishes his plate. He looks over at me. "Go for it."

"How come you don't have wings? Was your mother not a Wyern?" I ask, and the immediate way he goes still, looking away, I know I've hit a nerve. I all but blurt out the rest of my point. "I mean, you don't look exactly like Emerson or your father. I'm just wondering where you get the looks from."

His voice is sad and quiet. "My mother was a witch. Beautiful, immortal, and a leader of the witch clan, well, what is left of it."

I stumble for words, so many questions flickering around. "Witch clan? What is that?"

"Fae, Wyern, Siren and Witch were once clans, all bound to protect each other," he tells me. "I'm sure that past has been erased from your history books. The fae don't like anyone to remember how our races used to be equal and at peace."

I place my hand on his arm. "I'm sorry if I upset you. I just wanted to know you better."

He covers my hand on my arm. "Sometimes it's good to speak about the past, let it out of your chest with a friend. I don't remember my mother, other than in stories from my aunts. Her sisters who are still alive. My father beheaded her two months after I was born for tricking him into sleeping with her for a powerful heir. She might have been my biological mother, but she basically seduced my father, and that is wrong. What she did was wrong. My sister, Solandis, her mother was another witch doing the same my mother did. It wasn't so bad with Solandis as my father knew her mother for a long time and was an old friend."

My goddess.

"So it's the witch blood that makes you have no wings?"

"I had wings," he says quietly, his voice clipped and hoarse. Tears fill my eyes at the raw pain I hear. "I had wings… I was born with them."

"What happened?" I whisper in horror.

"Jealousy. Old, terrible magic and jealousy that ended with someone ripping my wings off. It was a punishment," he admits, his whole body shaking from the memory I've forced him to conjure up.

I put my hand over my mouth, sickness rising in my throat at even the thought. "How can you be so cheerful and kind after that happened to you?"

"Because if you let evil take over your heart, anyone that gets near you is tainted by it."

I wrap my arms around him from the side and hug him tightly. "I hope you got revenge."

"Not yet. But I will."

I hear the vow, and I hope he gets it. I'd love to help him, if that is even possible. He hugs me back and rests his head on top of mine. "You're a good hugger, mortal."

"You're my friend, Wyern."

I can feel him smiling even if I can't see it, and for a while, I just hug him and hope that it helps with the terrible memories.

I lift my head, finding him looking out of the window. "I feel like the goddess's sword is spinning our lives, weaving new fates for us, even as we speak. Do you feel it, mortal?"

"Do you really believe the old myths that once the goddess cut the world into existence with a sword and wove our lives in strands of string around it?"

"Yes," he breathes out. "We have our fate, Calliophe, and we cannot escape walking along our string."

For a moment, I wonder if he is right, and all of us are living a predestined life on the sharp blade of a magic sword.

CHAPTER
SEVENTEEN

The rest of the week passes by in a flurry of activity in M.A.D. thanks to three hybrid attacks, all seeming to be random, but two enforcers were killed taking them down. None of the hybrids were captured, and the random mortals they killed seem to be no one in particular or linked in any way that any of us could find. It's frustrating, and the symbol I found on the hybrid's back is not in the book anywhere, and Lorenzo told me his people haven't found anything on it. Which is odd, as he claims his libraries are older than even the fae's, so they should have a record of it.

I walk past a praying party. Twelve of them

are seated in a circle, holding an orange candle and praying to the goddess for the prince to be saved. I roll my eyes, knowing deep down that the goddess isn't going to listen to that prayer. In fact, very few will. The rumors spreading around the city about the Fae Prince being missing have swiftly changed to them assuming he is dead because of how long he has been gone. There hasn't been a royal funeral, or word from the Fae Queen, but people are expecting it.

People like these are mourning him already, and most of my colleagues have given up on finding him, even with the paycheck. I will not give up on him or the princess. I have this feeling that they are alive, and I'm going to find them. The answer is just out of my reach, but it's not impossible, and I've never given up on anything.

Wendy quietly calls hello as I head back into my office after lunch with Louie outside his school. I pause when I see the most gorgeous purple dress hanging on a hook on the wall. It's stunning, with a high neckline of shimmering material that would go around my neck and down my back and arms.

What is this dress doing in here? I walk in, touching the soft material and glancing back as the floorboard creaks. Merrick is at the door, looking at a paper in his hand, and he doesn't even look up for a moment. "Do you like the dress? The siren picked it."

"Nerelyth," I say to remind him of her name, "has brilliant taste."

"Good." He turns the paper over and keeps reading. "We're going into the fae district. Put it on."

"Why?" I ask.

It wasn't that I was against going there, because there could be a clue, but every time I've been in that place, it's so clear I don't belong. It's hard to think of anyone in my bloodline actually coming from there and somehow loving a mortal. Most of the fae really, really don't want mortals in their pretty district.

"There's a ball on tonight to celebrate some fae tradition of the Hollowing Star being at its highest point in the sky," he tells me, finally looking up from his paper. He meets my eyes with cool indifference. "The prince's girlfriend is going to be there, and she has agreed to speak with us. Only if we come and only for a few minutes. You best think quick on some questions for her."

I groan. "A ball, really?"

He pulls at the tie around his neck. "Trust me, I'd rather not be dressing up in a tux and going to this ball."

Sighing, I glance at the magic clock on the wall. "How long have we got?"

"Ten minutes, Miss Sprite. You best hurry."

I scowl at his back as he walks out, and I head over, shutting the door and locking it. Why is he taking me? I know I'm on this case, but there are so many much older and more qualified enforcers to take to the fae ball. I'm sure most of them wouldn't outright hate it there too.

I strip out of my clothes and slide into the dress before undoing my hair from the messy ponytail and grabbing my hairbrush from my drawers. After I've tamed my wavy locks, I easily do the buttons on the side of the dress until it's skintight against me. I have only a few minutes left when I dive into my drawer, rifling through various books, papers, pens and boxes until I find the small bag at the bottom I was looking for. I pull out the silver hair clip, bejeweled with silver flowers, that I found on the street ages ago and kept in here because it was pretty. I clip it in my hair, holding one side up, and pull my boots back on, easily hiding them under the skirts. I step into the strap for my thigh, clipping two daggers into it. Just in case. Can't be too safe around the fae.

I blow out a breath when I'm done and wish I had a mirror in here to see how I look before heading out of my office.

Wendy gasps. "You look like a princess, Miss Sprite!"

Heat crawls up my neck. "Thank you, Wendy."

"You're absolutely gorgeous," she replies with bright red cheeks and smiles big enough to brighten every shadow in the world. Sometimes I wish I could be like Wendy, so full of light and happiness, without letting the darkness around her taint her at all. She reminds me of Lorenzo, especially after our talk.

I may look nice here, to Wendy, but when I'm in a room full of fae females, I'm going to be the ugly duckling. I smile tightly before leaving and heading out into the bright sunlight, the heat of the day wrapping around me. Merrick has an enforcer carriage waiting, with a beautiful black horse pulling it, and he opens the door for me when I get there. "Pulling out the carriage? We must be on an important mission."

"Smartass," he grumbles as I climb inside, nearly tripping on the skirts of the dress, and now I remember why I don't wear dresses at work. Total trip hazard. Plus, it gives the monsters something to grab onto when I'm running away.

The door shuts behind Merrick with a hiss of magic, and the carriage takes off, led by magic we can't see or feel. Merrick kept his outfit simple, and I know he spent all of two minutes changing his jacket and tie into a bowtie, yet somehow it looks like a brand-new outfit. Crisp, efficient and everything I don't usually like about arrogant males. We females can spend hours doing our hair, makeup and wearing the perfect dress that cost a fortune, and males simply need a minute to run their fingers through their hair and throw on a three-piece suit.

I feel Merrick's eyes on me as I turn away,

looking out of the small window. "You look very beautiful, Miss Sprite."

"Thanks," I reply, my voice clipped.

"Have I upset you?"

I sigh and turn to him. "No, why would you ask that?"

"Since the—"

"Since the what? Work or date?" I arch an eyebrow. "I think neither of us knew, and I don't know how to deal with you."

"Date," he smoothly finishes his sentence. "You've all but disappeared on me. Tell me what is going on. I know there is something you're not telling me, and I can help you."

I struggle to keep the shock off my face. "There isn't anything. I'm just pissed you think that was a date when you never actually asked me out for anything but work."

He leans closer, his voice dropping. "Would you go on a date with me, Miss Sprite?"

My heart pounds. "No."

His eyes flicker with disappointment, and he leans back. "Why?"

My love life, by the goddess, it needs to be simple and monster/boss free. "My life is busy at the moment, and it wouldn't be a good idea to mix work with pleasure."

"Bullshit, Miss Sprite," he counters. "When you want to tell me the truth, you know where to find me."

I open my mouth to tell him something, anything, about what is really going on, when I see a boy about Louie's age sitting on the sidewalk, thin and pale, and clearly homeless. That would be Louie without me. I need the money I'd get from saving the princess and prince, and I need to get Louie and his mom out of this city. At least Louie is looking better now. His cheeks are filled out with weeks of eating decent food, and his hair shines, along with the new clothes we bought. Finally, no more holes or rips that I have to stitch up badly.

This is how he should have been looked after from the very start, and no child should be on the streets like that little boy. I won't let Louie ever become like that.

I feel like Merrick is analyzing my every word until we come to the fae district and the gates are open for us, the guards moving to the side. The carriage moves quicker throughout the fae district, which is silent until we come up a road that leads to the massive bronze gates to the castle road. We go past it and through a forest of sky-high trees before we come to an open field.

There's a gigantic white-framed greenhouse right in the center, pink flowers curling up all the sides, and there's a marquee tent at the back. The flawless grass lawn stretches for miles around it, filled in places with fae walking and sitting on benches, talking in groups, all of them holding drinks and wearing beautiful dresses or dark suits. Some part of me doesn't want to get out, stand next to them, and be compared. I bet the only mortals here are the waiters and staff, bound to the queen herself. Even then, there won't be many as the lower fae take the jobs in this district and look after their own.

I look at Merrick and nod once. This is work, and we can put our personal problems aside, just for now.

We need to know if she knows anything and get a general feel for her, if she would have a motive to do this or hire someone to. Merrick climbs out of the carriage when it stops, and offers me a hand, helping me into the grass before hooking my arm through his without another word. We walk across the soft grass lawn, several eyes turning our way. Some fae merely look, while some move directly in our path, forcing us to walk around them. To my surprise, some of the enchanting fae incline their head at Merrick, like they know him well, and he returns the gesture. Maybe the rumor about him being close to the Fae Queen isn't all rumor after all.

I ignore the blatant glances of disgust thrown my way as we near the greenhouse. A few fae head inside in front of us, blocking the view as we step inside and embrace the sticky heat of the room. We are both immediately offered pink sparkling drinks from a fae, who bows her head the entire time, and I see nothing but her brown hair and dark skin. I take the glass, needing a drink, and down one before putting the empty glass back. Merrick kindly refuses and flashes me an amused smile. "We are working, Miss Sprite."

I shrug a shoulder. "Just don't tell my boss."

That makes him laugh. "Why do I feel that is a regular saying for you?"

I grin because he is right, and it is. I look around the greenhouse, taking in every amazing part of it, until my mouth drops open. Every wall is made of glass, white rimmed around the edges, and tall trees take up every corner, the branches crawling up the glass. Beautiful different colored flowers shine on the branches like glitter, and the sweet smell in the room makes me wonder if it's from them. The center of the greenhouse is full of several little white tables and chairs. At the back of the room, there are fae dancing to a white-haired fae singing a soft song, music playing in the seven green fae lights hovering around her.

Merrick nods his head over to a female who is sitting with three other females, all of them stunning. "Emilana," he tells me. "The prince's favorite girlfriend. She comes from one of the most powerful families in the fae district and was favored to be princess and queen one day."

"Right," I say, watching them all. I could see why the prince would choose someone like her. Her blonde hair looks like it's pure sunlight wrapped up, and her yellow dress compliments her curves, thin waist, and sinful body.

Even her skin seems to glitter and sparkle as much as her blue eyes do. We both head over without another word, and I mentally remind myself to ignore the lure of the fae.

When we are a few feet away, she looks over, and her eyes flicker to me before scrunching her nose up in disgust. Typical fae. "You didn't say you were bringing anyone, Merrick Night. Especially not a fae bastard child."

"This is my partner, Calliophe Sprite," Merrick smoothly replies. "And her blood is of no concern to you."

She snorts and looks at her friends, continuing her conversation. Merrick clears his throat. "Five minutes. Remember?"

She rolls her eyes and clicks her fingers, and her friends walk away. Well-trained pups, it seems. "Out with it then. I don't want to be seen in the company of things like her for longer than necessary."

Ouch.

Merrick, ever the professional, places his hand on my back and carries on like she didn't just insult me. "We want to know if there's anything unusual that happened before he went missing. A jealous ex hanging about? Someone who threatened him in the weeks before?"

She laughs. "Jealous ex? There isn't a female here he hasn't fucked or tried to. By the queen, you'd struggle to find an unmated fae female that hasn't seen his cock."

Gross.

She sighs, looking at her pristine nails. "No one has ever been long-term except for me, and I wouldn't hurt him. Not ever. We understood each other."

I do believe that. He was her ticket to the throne.

"When did you last see him?" I ask.

She bristles at me before answering. "I saw him that night at the party. When the… hybrids came in, I was thrown across the room and knocked out. I didn't see him after that, and no one would dare to threaten the prince and live. He would have killed them for saying anything, or one of his personal guards would have."

I wonder if she's lying for just a second.

Not about all of it, but she is leaving something out. I can tell.

Before I can ask, she stands. "Excuse me, I have more dignified company to keep."

We both watch her walk away before I look to Merrick, and he takes my hand, leading me to the dance floor. He pulls me in the middle and places his hand around my waist before he starts moving us around to the same beat and dance as the other fae. I let him lead me along and ignore the pounding of my heart.

He leans closer, his voice but a whisper. "She was lying."

"I agree," I mutter.

He dips me in time to the music and spins me around before pulling me back into his arms. "I should have taken you dancing on our first date. Not our second."

I shake my head. "This isn't our second date, Merrick."

"It is," he replies firmly, and I chuckle, and he laughs with me, a surprisingly nice noise. Maybe he isn't all bossy, arrogant, and a general pain in my ass. We're laughing with each other, dancing around when there's a scream from outside.

Both of us pause mid step, along with every other person around us. The room stills as a second scream rings out, and my hand goes to my thigh, pulling up my dress and taking my dagger out.

Merrick and I make our way through the crowd and pause, looking through the glass to see five hybrids running straight across the lawn to us. They are pale, almost white-skinned, with black hands and feet and long bloody claws. In the distance, there is an outline of bodies, and I narrow my eyes. I'm about to run outside when Emilana steps out to the glass. Four males stand at her side, and all of them hold hands. Their eyes begin to glow white, like Emerson's do when he uses magic, and the glass shatters into nothing but white dust. Together they use their powers to make the ground beneath the earth shake hard under the hybrids, who all lose their footings, and two of them fall over before the earth cracks with a loud bang. The hybrids scream, the sound almost mortal, as they go down to the very bottom of the earth, and a gush of air throws the last three in before the earth slams shut, leaving the ground shaking. Emilana almost collapses. So do the males, and other fae rush to them.

"Impressive," I admit.

I barely get to look back when four more hybrids jump through the ceiling, and one slams right into me, his claws ripping down the back of my dress. I slam my dagger into its chest, using all my strength to push its horrible body off me, and I crawl to my knees as it coughs blood before going still.

Merrick already has his swords out, and he's fighting against two of them, beheading one effortlessly and cutting the legs off the other in one move before slamming his sword through its heart. I look over to see the fae have the last hybrid wrapped inside what looks like a hurricane of air, water and fire, the circle it's in getting smaller and smaller by the second. The hybrid looks up at me with dark hazel eyes through a small gap, and I'm sure it smiles in relief before it is burnt and suffocated by the water, and I have to look away.

They were mortal... once.

Merrick pulls me to my feet, and I clutch what is left of my dress around me tightly, trying to hide my back, my body, from the surrounding fae.

"Let's get you home," Merrick suggests, wrapping an arm around me. He speaks to a fae male, but I barely hear a word they say as I focus on not dropping my dress. "They can handle this, and the fae claim there aren't any more."

"Why here?" I question. Merrick understands what I'm asking, why the hybrids were attacking here, but he doesn't have that answer, and truthfully, none of us do. We head to the carriage, and he takes me right back to my apartment. I go to climb out, but his hand catches my arm, tugging me down. He leans in, kissing my cheek. "Thank you for another eventful date. Next time, we shouldn't invite our monster friends."

I can't help but laugh as I climb out. Merrick is insane. Feeling tired, I slowly pull myself up the hundreds of steps to my floor, a sigh of relief escaping my lips when I close the door behind me and I'm finally home. I don't know who is staying here tonight, but it is early yet, and I'm sure I have a little time to myself. A rare thing, at the moment.

I walk towards my bedroom, pausing to stand in the hall and look in the long mirror at myself. I let the dress fall, knowing it's exposing my back, and it falls in ribbons around me, the shoulders barely holding it up. I don't see him until he steps out of the shadows.

A monster at my back.

Emerson.

My heart pounds like a drum as his eyes take all of me in, and the hall feels small, too small for both of us, in this dim light.

I cautiously watch him in the mirror as he steps closer to me, my hands tightening on my lilac dress, the shimmering material bunching at my arms and waist.

His purple eyes never leave my back, and for a moment, I forget what is there to look at. Scars. I've had them since before I can remember, and they make up most of my back. Three long clawing scratch marks that start from my shoulders down to my hips. They are deep, ugly, and I hate that he is seeing them.

My breath hitches as he reaches out and softly runs his sharp-tipped nails down my back, over the scars, never once hurting me.

The Wyern King. The monster who kidnapped me... he is being gentle.

His eyes meet mine in the mirror, and his voice is lethal, dark and powerful. "Who the fuck did this to you?"

"I don't know," I admit. They are old scars, and I think they have been there since I was young, maybe even a baby. "Please don't look at them. They are horrible."

He steps closer, and he slowly kneels. I don't know what he is doing until he presses a kiss on my scar. "They show you are a survivor, and that is beautiful. Just as you are."

I close my eyes, tears filling them, and my throat feels tight as the king rises behind me. "Don't say that. Don't you realize that..."

"I can't stay away," he admits.

I nod. "Neither can I, but we have to. I'm mortal and you are the king of the Wyerns. We can't be together, Emerson, and every time you're around me, I fall a little more."

He is silent, and when I turn back, Emerson is gone, and the apartment is empty.

Tears fall freely as I want to slap myself for admitting that I'm falling for him, for saying anything at all. I throw the dress into the wash basket and pull on my pink silk pajama bottoms and silk cami top before going to my room.

I jump as a Flame appears on my bed, ash littering around him. He holds out a note. "From Nerelyth Mist."

"Thanks," I say, going back to the kitchen and getting a coin for him. He follows me and soon disappears after I chuck the coin his way. Sitting on the stool in the kitchen, I open the note from Nerelyth, which is a newspaper article.

"Gift to the Fae Prince by the sirens is the gift of magnetic power, to enhance his fire abilities. The two powers, while causing problems for the clocks and compasses in the fae district, will make for a powerful king. This gift only furthers the rocky alliance between sirens and fae."

The article goes on and on about the prince's other gifts, but I pause. Fire? Magnetic power? It all adds up. The Fae Prince wasn't kidnapped. He is behind all of this.

I hear the door being opened behind me, and I turn, expecting to see Emerson has come back.

But the hooded figure in the door isn't

Emerson. "Finally figured it out with a little help from your siren bitch friend?"

"Drop the hood, we both know who you are," I coldly reply, reaching for my hidden dagger under the counter.

He laughs right before he lunges for me, and the moment his warm hand touches my face, everything goes black.

CHAPTER
EIGHTEEN

Gleaming light flickers across my eyes, my head feeling groggy like a really terrible hangover as I blink a few times, a weird taste in my mouth. Fear intuitively takes over, making me shake from head to toe as I look across the gold-plated floor, realizing that the taste in my mouth is my blood mixed with magic, and I can feel it dripping from my nose onto my lip. The world is spinning, and it takes every inch of strength I have to pull my cheek from the floor where it was stuck. I'm still in my silk pajamas, and I rub the blood off my top lip and nose with my hand and blink a few times, not understanding where I am.

Until it hits me.

The scent in the air, the fae scent that hangs around this district. The Fae Prince brought me here... but why? I manage to pull myself up with a slight groan, every muscle burning, and I wonder how much magic or drugs he used to knock me out. I blink at the absolutely stunning room I'm in. Tall, arched, black-framed glass windows make up every single wall stretching up to the domed roof, lit with fae light shaped into wings that flit around continuously.

Outside the windows, I can see all of Ethereal City, and this must be the highest part of the city... which means it is the castle. It can't be anything else. It's night out, glistening stars lining the sky, but I know praying to them, to the goddess, is not going to save me. I draw my eyes back to the room, and I realize I'm not alone. But it's not the prince here.

Only a few feet away from me is the Fae Queen herself, in a massive green gown that pours over the throne she is sitting on. She's just as beautiful as I always imagined, her skin golden and her hair coiled up into a gold crown that matches the gold markings drawn down her arms. I recognize some of the fae symbols from the book I read. Mate. Fae. Control and some others I don't know.

She doesn't move, her empty expression never changing, but power radiates off her, and I know if anyone threatened her, she would kill them in seconds. She sits so silently, so still in the way the fae can be. Terror makes breathing hard as I kneel before the queen, not strong enough to even stand at this moment. The throne itself is magnificent, as I'd expect a throne made of melted gold to be. The seat has two butterfly wings spreading out the side, tiny sparkling fae lights falling off them onto the floor and spreading around the throne. I gulp, the pressure pounding in my head, and wipe my hand across my nose as more blood falls. I feel so weak.

Green chains are around my wrist, linked loosely together by a thin metal rope, and I don't know why he bothered chaining me. It's not like I have magic and they need to protect themselves from me. I'm mortal and I'm in the most dangerous place I can be for my kind. If I get out of here alive, it will be a miracle.

If I'm here, then the Fae Queen must know

about her grandson's crimes and everything he has done with the hybrids. That he was never missing, and she had us all looking for him to cover up his atrocities. The very queen looks down at me with her clear purple eyes, like gazing into a lake, but she doesn't say a word. Everything about her is perfect, and she is just as I thought she would be.

I don't know what to say, but I pull every bit of strength I have into focusing on standing up. I don't want to die on my knees, bowing to the Fae Queen who let this happen.

I barely manage to shakily stand, feeling sickness rising in my throat and my forehead lined with sweat when I hear footsteps and a dragging noise. The prince walks in from outside, one of the many gaps that lead to the wraparound balcony, dragging a bundle tied in rope. It takes me a minute with my blurry vision to see the bundle is a person, and she has dark wings.

The princess.

He drags her across the room and leaves her in front of the queen before turning to me, flashing me a pretty boy smile that just doesn't work. He is very handsome, his blond hair even brighter than his girlfriend's, and he is muscular under a crisp white shirt and dark trousers. He tucks his hands in his trousers, and I catch a glimpse of a gold blade strapped to his hip. If I can get that, then I stand a chance. I just need him closer.

His purple eyes roll over me. "Shall I break your legs so that you bow before your royals, mortal bitch?"

"Lovely," I snap.

He huffs and looks over his shoulder. "What do you think, grandmother? Oh right, nothing as usual."

The queen doesn't answer, but her eyes just stay locked on me, and I swear she is trying to tell me something. She looks like she hasn't moved in over a thousand years. I flash my eyes at Solandis, who isn't moving, blood pouring from a cut on the back of her head. "Did you kill her?"

"Well, you wouldn't like that, would you? Not when you've been working for Emerson to get her back. Did you know engaging with Wyerns against your queen is treason?"

"I was looking for you too," I remind him.

He smirks. "Well, I think Emerson might be pissed if you just brought back a body."

He kicks her once, my heart lurching, and she rolls over until she's facing me. I can see she's not dead, her chest is moving, but she's been severely beaten up. Black and blue bruises cover her until she's nearly unrecognizable. I look up at him and glare. "Why do it? Why make the hybrids? Why take her? What's the point of all this?"

"I do feel sorry for you," he taunts. "Never knowing any answers and asking all the questions, but no one telling you the truth. What will you give me to tell you my secrets?"

"Nothing," I bite out.

He flashes me a row of shiny teeth. "Shame."

He is in front of me in seconds, grabbing my chin roughly to the point I want to cry out in pain, but I won't give him the satisfaction. "I could break you so easily, mortal. Your blood would be so sweet."

"You're going to kill me, anyway. Why not tell me everything? Let's be honest." I stretch my hand out for the dagger, but it's just out of my reach. "You might as well tell me."

He reaches down and catches my hand, squeezing once, and the bones in my hand snap. I scream in pain, my knees going weak, and I barely hold myself up in his grip, scared he will break my face too. The Fae Prince looks deeply amused by this. I realize I don't even know his real name. No one does, and I can't even curse him when he does kill me. The Fae Prince and the Fae Queen don't tell anyone their name, only family.

"Going for this?" he asks, tutting. He pulls out a dagger from the side of him. A gold-plated dagger with strange symbols down the edge. Something draws me to it, pulling me closer, and I have to snap out of it to hear what he is talking about. "This is my inheritance. My dear dad's only unusual thing about his bloodline. There are creatures far worse than hybrids moving in the shadows, and they have been for a long time. We need an army to defend ourselves from the shadows, and a united world stood against them. We need a real king, not just that doll."

"She's your grandmother," I hiss in her defense.

"And she's nothing but a doll on a throne

controlled by petty people around her. I will be a king who rules alone, and I will take back the world we lost. We have been locked in our cities while the sirens control all the waters, the Wyerns control the mountains in the north, and the Hollow Lands are riddled with Snake Kind. When I'm king, we will expand our cities. No one will stand a chance against hybrids. Then, when the real threat comes, we will be ready."

He is insane. "You're mad."

"This dagger says otherwise. Only a true ruler can use it," he sneers. He flips it in his hand before removing his other hand from my chin, only to replace it with the tip of the dagger. "I could draw a fae symbol on your pretty skin and then watch you turn into a monster. Fitting end for a monster hunter, no?"

I push down my fear until there is nothing but calmness. "Then do it. I'm tired of listening to you."

He slaps me hard, and I fall to the floor with a smack, seeing black spots and barely resisting throwing up. It's not like I wasn't expecting it, but the hit was hard, and I'm so weak. My ears are ringing so much that I barely feel it as it starts, as darkness ripples into the room and the very ground shakes around us.

"Finally, he's got my message," the Fae Prince all but joyfully cheers.

He is a boy planning a party, and we are all just the guests with no say in what we are doing. He has planned it all. The prince strolls away from me like he hasn't got a care in the world and is over to the princess, picking her up by her wing and placing the dagger underneath her neck. I know who's coming even before he flies through one of the windows, smashing the glass to pieces and landing at my side.

Relief crawls up my chest as I clutch my hand over my heart. I look up at Emerson, but he barely glances at me, his foot inches away from my head. "The monster king finally comes back to save his dear sister and mortal toy. About time."

Emerson growls. "It's been you all along? You little fucker, I'm going to kill you."

The Fae Prince laughs as I feel Emerson's magic brushing against my skin, over my hand, and taking the pain away as he heals me. I almost sigh out loud, but I feel the prince's eyes on me, and I don't want him to know anything.

"We both know you can't. Cursed king."

Emerson still doesn't look at me, but he is tense, and the prince moves his eyes to me. "Shall I tell her the truth? Don't you feel bad for the poor mortal knowing nothing, not realizing she's been used all this time? That you wanted her to see if she could break the curse, and if she could, you'd kill her to do it."

"What are you going on about?" I demand, my heart racing in my chest and strength coming back to me. Emerson wouldn't use me, wouldn't kill me. It's not true.

"Oh sweetheart, you didn't think you could trust a monster?" the prince mocks. "For starters, did you know he is half fae and the true heir to the fae throne?"

"What?" I ask, my voice rattling.

"He's my uncle who betrayed us all. Selfish bastard," the prince taunts. Emerson is silent, and I want him to say something. I need him to say something.

Shock leaves me completely silent, and I

know the prince is loving this, my heart cracking slowly.

"What curse?" I snap.

"It's not her," Emerson growls.

"It is, you fool," the prince laughs. "You see, Emerson didn't want the crown all those years ago when he was meant to take it. He was brought up to take over both the Wyerns and fae, and unite our races by marrying a Siren Princess. His birth was planned by my grandmother and his father so they could finally have an heir to the world when his Wyern mate could not deliver one. But when he turned of age, he refused to marry the Siren Princess. Refused outright to be anywhere near her. So my grandmother lost control, and in anger, she cursed Emerson, his love and his court."

"Enough," Emerson demands.

"No, tell me," I demand, rising to my feet and refusing to look at Emerson at all when he finally turns my way.

"Wyerns don't always look like this, the monster you see now. They look like us, like fae usually, but they're cursed to be monsters permanently unless they manage to break the curse. They are also weaker, thanks to the curse. This power he shows now is but a tenth of how powerful he used to be. But there's no chance of that anymore, is there? Or so the king thought."

"Enough with the history lesson. Give my sister back now. You've had your fun," Emerson commands with a voice that should frighten the Fae Prince, but he doesn't even blink.

"You don't command me, king. The thing is, I'll stab this dagger through your sister's thin neck and use my dark shadows rippling under dear little Calliophe to swallow her whole before you even get to me. I think you'd have a chance to save one of them. Who would it be? I have a funny feeling it would be the poor, dear mortal at your side, even when you don't see who she is this time. How sad."

Emerson looks down at me, his eyes saying a million things, and my heart near enough stops just for him. He lied to me... but I still trust him more than the Fae Prince. "Then poor Calliophe would feel forever guilty that your sister died for her. Sad, sad times indeed."

"Fuck you," Emerson growls but his eyes are panicked.

The Fae Prince sighs. "Here's the deal. Make your choice quick before I get bored. I want you to declare now, with your blood, that you'll never claim the fae throne. That it is mine, and then you can take her and leave. I won't harm her."

Emerson looks tense, and I can see he doesn't want to do it. I'm not sure there is another way out of this. The prince has played us all too well. Emerson finally moves, striding over to the Fae Prince. "Fine. I never wanted this fucking throne in the first place. It's yours."

"In blood," the Fae Prince purrs. He lifts up a hand and quickly cuts his palm with one of his canine teeth, as sharp as Wyerns'. Emerson does the same before slamming his palm onto the prince's, dark green light bursting out of their joined hands. I swear the ground itself shakes under me right before the prince lets go of Solandis, and she falls to the floor. Emerson catches his sister, holding her up in his arms, turning around to me, only to find the prince is now at my side, the dagger underneath my neck now, and he laughs.

"I didn't say you could take both of them. You never do seem to listen, uncle."

Emerson is still, fury burning in his eyes, and his power fills the room. "Let her go."

"No," the Fae Prince replies. "We are old friends, Calliophe and me, and I think she deserves to know the truth about the curse and what it has to do with her."

"It's not fucking her!" Emerson shouts, his roar echoing around me, and I flinch.

I'm so scared I can barely breathe. The Fae Prince only keeps talking. "I can sense it every time you're born in the world."

"What are you talking about?" I whisper.

"There was once a sweet little mortal who worked in a palace full of fae. She fell in love with the heir to the throne, and he stole her heart away. On the day they were to be mated, the Fae Queen found out and used all of her power to cast a curse the world has never seen, leaving herself only a shell. The curse she wove cost the mortal her life that first time long ago. It was tragic, so I'm told, to see the once handsome prince turn into the monster he is now, along with his entire court and all Wyerns who serve him. They'll be monsters until he kills you but only if you love him first. That's the curse that she placed on you, on them, and that you would be reborn to give him several chances. I believe it went like this—

"Reborn to mortal life five times over,

Each time, a drop of power taken from the rift.

Monster cursed is her court,

Royalty protected is her fate,

She will be Queen of the Ruined Clan.

When twelve sit the throne,

She will be born at last.

No longer mortal will she be."

I can't breathe, the words floating around my mind, and they are somehow familiar. "But never once in your lifetimes did he get to you in time. You're destined to be star-crossed lovers by the curse. My grandmother was smart with magic borrowed from a witch queen, but she forgot that all great magic comes with a catch. The curse latched onto her daughter, making her linked to the mortal's life, and then when I was born, that curse fell on me. So we are linked, permanently, you and me."

My voice is hoarse. "Let me go."

"No," he breathes as I look at him and watch as his skin ripples into dark grey, and big wings spread out of his back, and his eyes turn dark. I know those eyes. I dream about them all the time. They haunt me.

He is the monster who hunted me.

Fear has me frozen as he steps behind me, wrapping an arm around my waist. "The first three times that you regenerated and came back, I managed to kill you as a child. The fourth time, he found you first. What a shame. Still, you died too soon. Killed by his own people before you could even love him. The fifth time, you stayed alive for a while, but he never found you before you drowned in an accident. This time I was so close, so many times, but the enforcers protected you, kept you safe. Some of them knew exactly what was happening and who you were. For some reason, they wanted you alive and made it damn near impossible for me to get to you. So you lived a sixth, impossible life. See, magic runs out, especially old magic. It always has a twist of its own. And when you turn sixteen, it makes it impossible for me to hurt you, to chase you anymore."

I look up at Emerson, who is still, and I swear he is afraid. My monster is afraid. "When you meet him, I begin to sense you again, and when you fall for him, I can hurt you once more. This time you chased me and made it so easy."

I'm speechless and shocked, but I don't look away from Emerson. I'm the person he was in love with, all those years ago, what he talked about in that room with Zurine.

"What do you want?" Emerson demands.

"To see you suffer, uncle," he purrs in my ear, his eyes on Emerson. "I want to make sure you can never touch my world when I'm king. She is perfect for that."

He holds up a vial in front of me with a long stabbing needle at the end. Inside, something shimmers purple, swirling fast like it's in a current of water. Like it's almost alive. "Do you know what this is?"

I shake my head, seeing Emerson put his sister down gently and jump in the air to me. A wall of fire appears around us, blocking him out.

"This will turn you into a fae or kill you. Ten percent chance of surviving. Good luck."

The Fae Prince holds me tightly as I try to fight him, and I can't stop him as he slides the needle into my neck. I scream in pain as he kisses my cheek, and I collapse in his arms, my body going weak.

"If you survive, then you'll be bound to me, my first fae, and you'll never be able to resist my command. You'll be mine."

The last thing I hear is a monster's roar before I see nothing but glittering stars.

Printed in Great Britain
by Amazon